MW01029418

# A Powerless World

## Book 1

# When the Power is Gone

### P.A. Glaspy

Originally self-published by P.A. Glaspy in 2016

Published by Vulpine Press in the United Kingdom in 2017

Cover by Claire Townsend

ISBN: 978-1-910780-44-2

www.vulpine-press.com

For Jim, my husband, my confidante, my cheerleader, and my best friend. I could not have done this without you.

# Chapter 1

The digital clock on the microwave read 7:15. Late again.

"Russell Gordon Mathews! If you aren't down those stairs in five minutes, you will miss the bus *again*, and this time you'll be *walking* to school, because I do *not* have time to take you this morning, because *I'm* late for work now from trying to get *you* out the door on time!" Yes, it was a really long rant, but I was frustrated to no end. My son had stayed up late playing games online with his friends, and now he was paying the price for not getting enough sleep. And I was paying the price as well. And it was Monday.

My husband, Russ Sr., was on his way home from an emergency call for his maintenance business. Being in business for yourself has its perks, like setting your own hours, but loyal customers like Marietta, who had called at 4:00 a.m. with a busted pipe in her bathroom, garner some favor. Marietta Sampson was a well-to-do widow whose husband had left her a boatload of money, and she only lived about ten miles away. She was completely clueless when it came to how to actually "do" things. She was Russ's number one customer. I think she might have had other designs on my hardworking, handsome husband, but he was oblivious to this aspect of their relationship. Just one of the things I loved about him—he was clueless.

Rusty finally came down, dragging his backpack behind him. With his electric toothbrush still going in his mouth and his iPod buds in his ears, he was the epitome of a twenty-first-century teenager. Months away from being able to get his driver's license, he was dependent on the generosity and goodwill of his parents to get anywhere without walking or riding his bike, which he had just recently gotten "too big" to ride. Right then, my goodwill was nonexistent. He could just consider himself a walking-everywhere kid for making me late … again.

"Mom, I need—"

"What you need is to get out that door and on the bus, now!"

"But Mom, I really need it!"

My cell phone started buzzing. "Need what?" I shot back while checking the caller ID. It was Russ, calling to let me know he was almost home, I was sure. Good, he could deal with this kid. I was so late for work. I held up a finger, signaling Rusty to stop talking while I answered the phone. A finger and a mom look got me the silence I was looking for.

"Hey, baby," I said. Everything okay?" I checked the clock on the microwave again. 7:25. Crap. I was going to get a load of grief when I got to work.

"Hi, honey. Yeah, all good. I'll be home in five minutes. Is Rusty out waiting for the bus?"

"He's walking out the door *right now*." I gave my son a look that could have taken out a small village. He looked at me with some frustration of his own—I'm sure because he never got to tell me what it was he needed—then headed for the front door, walking dejectedly.

Laughing over the line, Russ said, "Okay, I'm turning down our street now. I'll—" The call cut off, just as the lights went out, the compressor on the fridge stopped, and the displays on the microwave and oven went dark.

"Russ? Baby? You there?" I looked at my phone; it was off. I pressed the power button, but nothing happened. I had just charged it the night before, so I knew the battery was good. I had a sinking feeling that I knew what this was, but I did not want it to be true. To test my theory, I rushed over to the table and tried to start my laptop. Nothing. My tablet was the same. Nothing electronic was working.

Yep, I knew exactly what this was. And it was going to really suck.

It was an EMP, or electromagnetic pulse, which fries everything electronic, or so the doomsday preppers said. Guess what? They were right. Dammit.

Rusty was looking at his iPod in confusion. "Mom? I charged my iPod last night while I was sleeping. It's dead. I'm going to need a new one." He had no idea what had happened—yet.

"Rusty, shut the door. You're not going to school." His hooray would be short-lived when he found out nothing was working, and why. My twenty-first-century kid was about to get a history lesson—specifically, what life was like before electricity.

Yep, *really* gonna suck.

I went to the garage and tried to start my SUV. No joy. My 2012 Ford Escape was too new, with too many computer chips. I think the salesman had beamed over it having like thirty-two of them. *No help to me now, dude.* As I was heading back into the house, I heard Russ pull into the driveway in his 1980 Dodge pickup. His beater work truck, which had no computer chips, was running fine. He'd been right when he said it would run if this happened. So, two doomsday questions answered: nothing new and reliant on electricity worked, but old stuff—not so "modernized"—did.

Russ burst through the front door. "Is everything down?"

I looked at him with what I knew was an expression of dread. "Yeah, anything with a chip, or that was plugged into the grid." I was not happy to report it, but he had come to the same conclusion I had. One of the things we had hoped wouldn't happen, but had planned against, was coming to life right before our eyes. The lists started in both our heads. What we needed to do, when we needed to do it, and where we would be going now.

There was some kind of—I don't know what it was—commotion outside. The house shook, as if there had been an explosion, but there was nothing else. We rushed to the door and out into the yard. No noise, no fire—we had no idea what it was. Right then, it wasn't a priority. Our immediate future was priority number one, and as long as whatever it was didn't touch us, we had more important things to worry about.

My husband looked at us both with a face full of resolve. "We know what we have to do. Let's get inside and get started."

\*\*\*\*

About three years ago, Russ and I had a "come to Jesus" meeting regarding preparing for disaster scenarios. I was going along in my day-to-day life, looking no further into the future than what we would have for supper that week. We could have made it maybe a week to ten days off the food we had in the house, including the freezer. There was no long-term planning for even a short-term disaster. If the power went off and the outage lasted more than a day, we would be having a big cookout, because the freezer held most of the meat we had. A couple of cases of bottled water in the pantry were the only water stores in the house.

Whenever Russ tried to bring up "prepping," I would shudder at the thought and try to change the subject. All I could think of was a bunch of mountain people holed up in a cabin on a hilltop with no running water, no bathroom, but lots of kids and guns. I knew nothing about it, and wasn't really interested in learning more. I couldn't fathom losing modern conveniences, like internet, electricity, and running water, for more than a few hours. It just didn't happen.

We had a couple of handguns and a couple of shotguns in the house, with maybe two hundred rounds of ammunition for all of them. I knew my way around guns, and actually enjoyed shooting, but I never looked at them as "survival" tools. I considered them self-defense tools, nothing more. If anyone broke into our house in the middle of the night, they were in for a bad experience, as we both had a pistol in our bedside nightstands.

Russ persisted, sending me links to blogs of people theorizing all sorts of doomsday scenarios. At first, I was completely skeptical. No way any of these things could happen. An economic collapse? We'd know way in advance if that were coming, and the government would help us get through it. No, the irony is not lost on me now that my thought process did not take into consideration that the government would be the cause of that particular one.

A foreign invasion, taking our country into war on our own soil? Again, my thought was that the government would take care of that. That's their job, right? They command the troops. They control the money. They wouldn't need me meddling in their affairs, and whatever they did wouldn't affect my day-to-day life. I lived in Tennessee, for God's sake. No one attacks Tennessee. What were they going to do, invade Dollywood? Camp out on the lawn of the Hermitage? Take up residence at Graceland? Yes, I was very naive.

The EMP was the one I thought least likely to happen. Surely the government—yes, still on that path at the time—had considered this as an option, and was prepared for such an unlikely event. They would make sure we didn't lose our precious utilities, no matter what happened.

As I read more and more opinions on the matter, however, the dull light bulb in my brain kept getting a little bit brighter with each passing theory. Maybe it could happen. Any of them. To combat my confidence in the government, Russ only had to remind me of one thing—Hurricane Katrina.

While those of us living in middle Tennessee only had to deal with heavy rain, the citizens of New Orleans lost everything. The people were stranded on their roofs, or in their flooded homes for days and days—no power, no clean drinking water, no food, no emergency services—while a stunned local and federal government sat around trying to figure out what to do. When they did finally start into the flood-ravaged neighborhoods, they declared martial law—and went about confiscating everyone's firearms first thing. You know, for everyone's safety. Now, not only did the people not have a decent home anymore, they were suddenly left defenseless against looters, rapists, pretty much every level of lowlife that slithers out of the chaos of a catastrophe to prey upon innocent people. Lawlessness was rampant, and many people were killed, both during the flood and after. It took months for some of the people to get any sense of normalcy, and others lost everything, never to get it back.

When the light bulb finally went full-on bright, Russ had his partner in this venture—we were going to start prepping. The more I thought about it, the more it made sense. Even if none of the shit-hit-the-fan scenarios happened, what if a tornado came through and wiped out the town? How would we survive? There was a major flood in Nashville in 2010. Thousands of people were flooded out of their homes. What would you do if the grocery stores in the area were closed due to flooding? How would you get to those in higher, drier sections of town if your car was under water? If you could get food, where would you keep it, if your home was uninhabitable? These kinds of thoughts were on my mind every time I turned around. That old saying, "It's better to have it and not need it than to need it and not have it," was my motto. I got it. Now, what was I going to do about it?

We started small. I bought a twenty-pound bag of rice and twenty pounds of pinto beans. We could live for months with those two items as our food. It would get old, but we could eat. Next was water. Over the next few weeks, we added ten cases of it to our stores. You could get a twenty-four-bottle case for less than three bucks. Two or three a week picked up at the grocery store for less than ten dollars added up fast.

I was really starting to think about all the things we could use or need in an emergency situation. I went to the local wholesale store and bought flour and sugar in twenty-five-pound bags. I bought food-grade five-gallon buckets online to store them in. Mylar bags with oxygen absorbers gave me a sense of security that I could store these items long term, and the buckets would withstand water and sunlight—two big issues in keeping emergency food stores. To buy the things you need to survive in a disaster, you have to have a large surplus, but some food items have a short shelf life, so you have to plan accordingly. I tried to work on items that would last longer, like freeze-dried foods with a thirty-year shelf life. If I lived that long, and nothing happened, I'd test that longevity statement. For now, I was relying on the claims being truthful. Even if the food lost some of its flavor or nutritional value, you could still eat it. It might taste like ass, but you could survive on it.

I added items I thought would be something we could eat in an emergency situation, and would break up what would quickly become monotonous for at least twice-daily meals. Oatmeal, dried milk, crackers, peanut butter, honey, tuna—I chose things that could be eaten without cooking as often as I could. Honey is one of those foods that never go bad and can be used for lots of things, so there was lots of that. Protein would be needed for energy, to do whatever we needed to do to live in any doomsday scenario, and unopened peanut butter and tuna last well past their "best if used by" date. That theory I had tested.

We set a budget for "preps" of two hundred dollars a month. I tried to do at least that. Within a couple of years, we had a ten-by-ten spare room (formerly known as my craft room) half full of supplies. Besides food and water, we had first aid items, including extra meds of prescriptions and veterinary antibiotics (no prescription needed); extra toothbrushes and toothpaste, soap, antibacterial gel and wipes; *lots* of toilet paper and feminine products; batteries, candles, seed banks, yards of material (from when it was a craft room), books on survival—truly anything I could think of that might be useful, as well as hard, if not impossible, to get if the world went down the toilet. No pun intended, but I'm pretty sure Charmin and Angel Soft were not going to be readily available when the SHTF. We started keeping chickens and rabbits in our backyard. We had a couple of raised bed gardens where we grew veggies for us and the critters. Our privacy fence did a good job of keeping the critters safe and keeping the neighbors in the dark—except for the Hoppers.

We had met our neighbors from next door when our kids were in grade school. Bob and Janet Hopper had been our best friends for ten years. They had a son, Ben, who was the same age as Rusty, and the two were like brothers. When we decided to go down the path of prepping, it was a natural progression to include them in our plans. As an established prepper, I was concerned they'd think we were whack jobs. A couple of years ago, if the shoe had been on the other foot, I would have thought that about them. I worried needlessly. Bob and Russ were like brothers from another mother, because they were so much alike. Bob immediately saw what Russ had worked so hard to get me to see. Janet was skeptical like me, in the beginning, but as a stay-at-home mom who had grown up spending summers at her uncle's farm, she was much more knowledgeable about a lot of the things we were trying to do than I was. In a very short time, their preps were as deep as ours. Our disaster plan, no matter what the scenario, included them. End of discussion.

Next question: how were we going to make sure some douchebags didn't come kick in the door and take all of our hard-earned preps? We lived in a rural neighborhood—that is, we had neighbors across the street, but with a half-acre of front yard on each place, it was a walk to get there. That was the layout of the whole street. Close, but not too close. The problem was that big, open front yard. With a few trees for shade, it wasn't really a defensible location. There was about a half-acre between our house and the Hoppers'.

When Russ first brought up defense, I kind of rolled my eyes. Really? You think people would just come kick in our door to get our stuff? Decent people don't act like that, and I truly believed most people were just that—decent. Then there were riots in

Ferguson, MO. Then Boston. Guess what? People were going around kicking in doors and windows and taking other people's stuff. So we bought guns. Handguns, both revolvers and pistols; shotguns, in 12- and 20-gauge; rifles in just about every caliber there is. And ammo—oh, the boxes and boxes of ammo. Thousands of rounds, hundreds in each caliber, at a minimum. And of course, Bob and Janet did as well. We had multiple firearms that would shoot the same bullets among all of us.

Everybody learned to shoot. We spent hours at the range with different handguns and rifles, until all of us, including the boys, were comfortable with loading, unloading, shooting, cleaning, safety application—the works. All of the adults had handgun carry permits as well. We didn't go anywhere unarmed. We also didn't go anywhere that posted "No Guns Allowed." The world was a dangerous place, and the cops always got there in time to draw chalk outlines and take witness statements. We would not willingly put ourselves in a position to be victims, because here's the problem: bad guys don't care if you have a sign. They still come in, with guns, sometimes out and shooting, and all the law-abiding citizens didn't bring their lawfully owned and legal-to-carry sidearms in with them because of your stupid sign, so there's no one to shoot back. And now, they are among the wounded or dead, as well as your other customers and employees. Dumb asses.

The biggest part of our survival plan kind of happened by accident. Janet's uncle was getting on in years, but wouldn't leave his farm. As Janet was his only surviving relative, Uncle Monroe Warren signed over the deed to his twenty-acre farm to Janet and Bob a couple of years ago. His only stipulation was that he and his wife, Millie, would get to live out their days on the farm, and that they would be buried side by side on the hill behind the house. For that, they would keep the farm going, with our help and that of a couple of the neighbor's boys. We went to the farm at least every other weekend. We made sure we had established gardens, with every vegetable we could think of to grow. Millie had always lived on a farm, and lived off of the land as a child, with her family. She knew how to grow and store pretty much anything we planted. We had all kinds of livestock, both for food and working animals, and a herd of big dogs, who loved us all and were fiercely protective of the folks and the place.

We kept the large farmhouse in good order. Monroe had built the house when he was young, right after he and Millie got married, expecting a large family. Fate kept that from happening. Monroe was kicked by a horse he was trying to shoe, and the wound left him sterile. He and Millie never had children, but they filled that big six-bedroom house with love. As a child, Janet would beg to spend the whole summer out there. Aunt Millie kept her busy, but Janet didn't see it as work. She thought it was fun. Ah, kids. Millie was still quite feisty, and when we first started going out there with Bob and Janet on the weekends, just to get away, she mothered and grandmothered all of us. I couldn't have loved and cared for them more if they had been my blood. They were country people, who had lived through hard times, and they were a wealth of knowledge on what we were doing. Millie had a root cellar filled top to bottom with home-canned goods, root vegetables, old metal cans full of flour and sugar, boxes of salt; the list of food items was long. They also had kerosene lanterns, candles, cast iron cookware that had seen more than its share of open-pit cooking, as well as country hams hanging and a butter churn. Seriously, a for-real pump-the-dasher-up-and-down butter churn. Millie said it had belonged to her mother, and that yes, it still worked.

When we told them what we were doing, they smiled at us, then each other. Millie said, "Well, it sounds like we've been preppers for a long time." She was right. If everything went down, the only way they'd have known is the lights wouldn't work. They had a wood-burning stove, fireplaces, lanterns—they were set up perfectly for what we would need if the world went to hell.

The farm was thirty miles away. We could get there in forty-five minutes to an hour, barring any traffic problems. This was our bug out location. In the event we could not stay in our homes, after no more than thirty days, this was where we would go.

# Chapter 2

As we were going over what needed to be done and trying to prioritize everything, there was an incessant knocking at the front door. I looked through the security peephole and saw Janet. I opened the door, and she burst in, tears flowing.

"Anne, my God, this is it, isn't it? Nothing electric is working. It's all dead. What do we do now?" Janet was an emotional sort, but right then, I was feeling almost as overwhelmed as she looked. She was followed by Ben, who was still carrying his school backpack.

"The bus didn't show, and I guess now it won't," he said, more to Rusty than anyone else. Both of our sons had been involved in our planning for this sort of situation. They understood as well as we did what was happening, although right now they were a little too happy about not going to school. They'd get over that. I had a feeling that in the upcoming months they would wish for a boring day at school over the daily grind of just living without any modern conveniences.

"Where's Bob?" I asked Janet, hoping the answer wasn't what I was afraid it was going to be. Bob was a computer tech at a big electronics store in town. If he was at work already, he was fifteen miles away, with a car that no longer ran. Their bug out vehicle was in their garage.

"He left about five minutes before everything went off. He's probably about five miles away, if traffic wasn't bad." Janet was pacing the kitchen like a caged animal.

Russ chimed in. "Right before it went off, the radio was on a local station, doing a traffic update. Said it was backed up from Pine Haven all the way to the interstate from an accident. No way he was even on the interstate yet. He should be walking up in the next hour, no longer. He has his get home bag in his car, and his pistol on his side. Don't worry, he'll be here. We have work to do while we wait."

A get home bag, or GHB, is a bag you keep in your car that has supplies to get you home from wherever you are if something like this happens. Usually, it has food and water for about seventy-two hours, along with a first aid kit, Mylar blanket, emergency flares, whistle, flashlight—preferably wind up. The list is completely adaptable to the person and the situation. I for one have an extra pair of underwear and socks in mine. A gal has to have priorities, and dry socks and drawers are some of mine. Oh, and feminine products. It would suck *really* bad to get caught away from home for a few days and have your monthly visitor show up. Bob probably wouldn't even have to dip into his for anything other than water.

Russ knew getting Janet focused on what lay ahead was the best thing right then. Just the words spoken seemed to calm her down, and I could see the resolve in her eyes. "You're right, Russ. The more we have done before he gets home, the less he'll have to do when he gets back." She even graced us with a small smile.

"First thing we do is check to see if the Faraday cages actually worked," Russ said. "Those electronics will make our immediate future easier, and our long-term survival better." Russ was right again. We had invested some money and energy in electronics, in the hope we could protect them from this very thing. I was anxious, but excited to find out if the electronic devices we had tried to protect from an EMP were still functional. We all headed to the prep room.

A Faraday cage is a metal enclosure, built to surround electronic devices and protect them from an EMP. The premise is that the enclosure will absorb the pulse, as long as the electronics are insulated from the metal. This can be done with paper—doubtful, but maybe if they were wrapped in aluminum foil around the paper; or cardboard—probable; or possibly even anti-static bags. I say possibly because, in the prepper community, there is still a lot of speculation as to whether this would actually work. The small Faraday cages were lined with cardboard and each of the electronic devices was inside an anti-static bag. Bob worked at an electronics store, remember? We had plenty of bags.

Russ and Bob had read everything they could find on them, but in the end it was always going to be a hope and a prayer. They built them out of metal ammo cans for small electronics like e-readers and two-way radios, and metal cabinets for the electric hand tools and generators. The ammo cans were in the prep room and housed e-readers and small tablets with a lot of survival books loaded on them, as well as two-way and emergency, multi-band radios. Everything from urban gardening and backyard animals to identifying edible plants in the wild and basic first aid was loaded on the e-readers. They would definitely help us survive in the coming days, weeks, months—hell, it could be years.

Russ pulled out the first can, the one with my e-readers and mini tablet. As he opened it up, I said a quick prayer. Aside from the survival books, I had over a thousand novels on one of them. With no TV, radio, or internet, having a thousand books on a small handheld device would definitely help to pass the time, and save a lot of space. He handed me the e-reader on top. "You loaded it up, you get to do the honors."

I took it, closed my eyes, and flipped the cover open. The screen lit up! "Oh my God! *It worked, it worked, oh my God!*" I was screaming, and dancing around the room, and everyone else was grinning and high fiving each other. The boys were particularly pleased, because there were at least some games on the tablet to occupy their time. First test: success!

We put everything back in the can after we tested each item. We checked the other cans with radios, both emergency and two-way, a cheap pre-paid cell—who knows, maybe you could send a text—and a handheld ham radio. We verified they'd survived, then packaged them back up, just in case. Who knew if there might be a secondary pulse? We didn't want to get sloppy right out of the gate.

Since the small cans had worked, Russ was antsy to check the cabinet in the garage. A working generator would increase the time our cold-stored foods would be edible. The longer we could go without breaking into our long-term food stores, the longer they would last. We all trekked out toward the garage.

As we were going out the kitchen door, there was an incessant knock at the front door. Rusty started that way, but Russ stopped him. "Beginning right now, no one goes out of the house alone. No one even goes to the door alone. And everyone starts wearing their sidearms, even you boys." Russ grabbed his from the kitchen counter, where he had laid it when he came in. He went to the door, with all of us around the corner, and looked out the peephole. He turned around with a grin, looked at Janet, and said, "I think it's for you."

Janet looked confused for a moment, then squealed and ran to the door. She jerked it open, squealed again, and jumped into Bob's arms. Bob picked her up, carried her inside, and we joined in a round of hugs, handshakes, and back slaps.

"Oh, honey, you made it home! I was so worried!" Janet was laughing and crying at the same time.

Bob grinned at her and said, "Sugar, you should have known nothing would keep me away from you and Benny." Ben grimaced at the "little boy" name his dad still used from time to time, but couldn't hide the happiness and relief he felt that his dad was home.

Russ stepped in, looked at Bob with a serious expression, and laid his hand on Bob's shoulder. "We checked the small Faraday cages, Bob."

Bob took on an equally serious and slightly pained expression. "What? They didn't work?" Bob would have taken that as a personal failure, since he was the electronics geek and had done more research than anyone on how to build one that would actually, hopefully, work.

Russ looked down at the floor, and back up at Bob with a smart-ass smirk. "They worked great. We were just going to the garage to check the big one. Let's go, buddy."

Bob turned his frown upside down, smacked Russ on the back of the head, and headed for the garage. "Asshole." That was a term of endearment between these guys. We went to the garage and stood before the cabinet like it was a shrine. This was a big deal.

"Bob, since you missed the appetizers, you can open the main course," Russ said.

Bob grinned again, took a deep breath, made the sign of the cross—and he is *not* Catholic—and reached for the handles. We all took a deep breath with him, and pretty much held it as the doors opened. The first thing Bob grabbed was an electronic volt meter. If that functioned, the rest of the equipment had a good chance of working as well.

He flipped the switch, and the display lit up. "Yeah! Alright!" Bob was fist pumping the air, while the rest of us did another round of hugs and high fives. We had electronics and power. This life-changing day was starting to take a turn for the better.

We were all feeling pretty good about the direction things were going and talking about how to utilize the protected electronics when there was another knock at the front door. Everybody we needed to worry about was here. So, who was it?

**\*\*\*\***

Russ and Bob both had their sidearms on them—Russ from earlier, and Bob from his trek home. His gun and his GHB were always with him when he went back and forth to work, just like Russ and me. Prepping 101: your preps mean nothing if you can't get to them. Russ told the rest of us to stay in the kitchen while he and Bob went to the door. He looked through the peephole, then turned around and mouthed the word "Brian." I think we all rolled our eyes at once.

Brian was the snooty neighbor from the other side. He was single, probably because he was annoying as hell and full of himself. He had the latest and greatest of every gadget out there, the most technologically advanced available. He was some kind of financial planner, so he kept bankers' hours and wouldn't have left for work yet. He had a look of complete confusion on his face when Russ opened the door. He was wearing a suit and tie and holding his phone in his hand.

"Hi, Brian. What can I do for you?" Russ was starting with polite. I knew it wouldn't last. He couldn't stand Brian.

"Yo, mornin', Russ. Say, is your power out? Everything just shut off a while ago. Funny thing is, my phone isn't working, which is weird, right? I thought maybe the battery went dead, so I went to my car to try the charger and my car is dead too. I mean, what the hell, man? How could everything be dead?" The whole time he was talking, he was pushing the power button on his smartphone, as if one of the attempts would be the magic one that turned his precious lifeline back on. Pitiful. But then, a few years ago, that would have been me. Before I took the red pill.

Russ covered up a sigh, looked Brian in the eye, and nodded. "Yep, all ours are down too. The whole neighborhood is out." Russ had decided to try playing dumb.

While Brian was an ass, he wasn't a dumb ass. He looked at Russ, looked over at Russ's truck in the driveway, then back at Russ. "Didn't I hear you drive up in your truck right after everything went off? Is your truck still running? Why is your truck running but not my car? I mean, my car is state of the art. Can you give me a ride into the office? I have a big meeting at ten, and I really need to be there for it. It would really help me out, man." Brian was carrying on the conversation with himself, because, well, in his mind, the world revolved around him and his needs. I looked at Russ, who was losing the fight with himself to not slam the door in Brian's face, no explanation, just done. We had things we needed to be doing, and dealing with Brian was not on the list.

Russ looked at me, gave me a slight nod, and turned back to Brian. The nod said, "I'm giving him the condensed version, then getting rid of him." Yep, we were that close—I knew what he was thinking.

"Look, Brian, I'm going to try to explain to you what I think is going on, so be quiet and listen. I believe we have been hit with an EMP, which—" was as far as he got before Brian interrupted him.

"What the hell is an EMP?"

Russ took a deep breath, and started again. "As I said, I will try to explain, but you need to shut up and *listen*." He looked at Brian, waiting to see if he would comply; when he didn't say anything, Russ continued. "An EMP is an electromagnetic pulse. It can be created by detonating a bomb in the atmosphere, or even by a sun spot exploding. When that happens, anything with a computer chip in it, or anything electronic plugged into an electrical outlet, will probably be rendered unusable. Since most appliances and all devices like cell phones and laptops have computer chips in them, they are all toast now. New cars have tons of computer chips in them, so those are garbage now as well. The reason your car doesn't run is it is full of chips. The reason my truck does run, is it was built before cars had computer chips in them. Life as you know it is pretty much over." Russ stopped to see how Brian was dealing with all this information. Brian had the deer in the headlights look big time. He didn't speak, so Russ continued.

"No, I can't take you to your office. I guarantee you that meeting is canceled. No one will be going to work again for a while, at least not a regular job in an office. You have a new job now, called surviving. It will take everything you have, everything you are, to live now. I can help you with that, just a little. I can give you some advice and hope you take heed to what I tell you." Russ stopped again, making sure Brian was still listening. He shouldn't have worried—he had the full attention of not just Brian, but all of us. This was the discussion we would have had with the kids had we not been interrupted by Brian. Not that they didn't already know it, but it deserved a refresher course.

"The first thing you need to do is fill every sink and tub in your house with water, while it's still running. It won't be for long—when the system is emptied, it will be gone. Anne? Speaking of water …" Russ looked at me, and I knew what he was talking about. I nodded and turned to Janet.

"Right. Janet, can you handle that? I want the boys to hear what Russ is saying." Janet nodded and went off to fill the water-BOBs in our tubs.

A waterBOB is a large bladder that will hold a hundred gallons of water. You put it in the tub, fill it from the faucet, and it will keep water for up to three months. It comes with a hand pump to get the water out of the bladder. Once ours were full, we'd head to her house and fill theirs as well. Russ was right; computer chips kept the water moving. Those had been fried with all the others. Welcome to the new world. It was going to suck. Did I already say that?

Russ turned back to Brian. "After that, you need to go to the store on the corner. I hope you have some cash on you, because your credit cards are worthless pieces of plastic now. Buy all the food you can carry. Don't buy stupid things like frozen dinners. You have no way to keep them frozen and no way to cook them, either. You can buy bread, but not a lot, not more than you could eat in a week. It will go bad after that. Buy peanut butter and crackers. Buy canned food you can eat cold if you have to. Buy tuna and ramen noodles. If you don't have a way to cook other than your electric stove, I'll help you build a rocket stove. It's a small stove built out of a can that produces a lot of heat with just a few sticks. Water is the most important thing, then food. Understand?" He looked at Brian, who was still wide eyed, but nodding slowly.

"Do you have a gun?" Russ asked, looking him in the eye. Brian hesitated, but finally nodded in the affirmative. He still didn't speak. Russ gave a slight nod himself, and said, "Good. You need to start keeping it with you at all times. Lock your doors, and don't let anyone in—I was going to say unless you know them, but you shouldn't let anyone in, period. People get desperate when they get hungry, and there are going to be a lot of hungry people out there in just a few days. Most people don't have enough food in their homes to last a week, and this is going to last a lot longer than that. People with kids are even more dangerous, because parents will do anything to take care of their kids. Don't fall for the 'do you have a little something you can spare for my kids' line. If they find out you have any food, they will come in to take it all. Yes, you will feel like a dick, but you'll be a living dick." Russ paused again. I think he was worried Brian would have a stroke or something from information overload. Brian just kept staring at him, still quiet.

"I can't give you all the information you need, Brian. I have to start getting my family prepared for the coming days. I will tell you this—do not come back here. In the next couple of days, we will be locking down our home and the Hoppers', and no one will be allowed in. We will be responding to anyone who knocks on the door with a drawn gun in hand. It's going to get bad, and it's going to happen pretty fast. I would suggest that, if you manage to make it a couple of weeks, you try to walk out to somewhere with resources. I don't know where that will be. I don't care. We should be gone by then. I can't stress to you enough how important it is that you keep your gun on you. There will be bad people out there soon. After the looters have cleaned out all the food in the stores, then they will go through apartments, houses, and condos in the city. After that, they'll work their way out to the suburbs, then further and further, to places like this. They will be criminals who have no conscience, and there will be no consequences for their actions, since the police won't be working either. They will kill you for a can of Spam and not think twice about it. If you have any questions, now is the time to ask them." Russ paused, giving Brian a chance to speak, now that he had been given permission.

Brian looked like he might laugh or cry, I couldn't tell which. He looked at Russ, and in almost a whisper said, "Russ, are you sure about this? Is this really what happened? What's happening? Could you be wrong? Dear God, is this for real?" Cry it was, then. I was shocked. I'd thought Brian would be too into himself and technology to believe it. Apparently not. He rose a few steps in my esteem that morning.

"Yes, it's true. It's the only explanation for everything going down at once. You need to go home now, change into some durable clothes and get busy. Do you want me to help you build a stove to cook on? You need to make plans for a toilet replacement too. If you have a five-gallon bucket, I can help you with that while I'm there." So many people forget about the toilet. If there's no water, there's no flushing. Even if you can flush for a while, eventually the sewers back up and … yeah, that. Nasty, and dangerous. Disease and germ heaven, sanitation hell. I tried hard not to think about that particular item. I mean, the guys can go out back and pee on the fence. Us gals need to have a toilet option when the time comes.

Brian took a deep breath, stood up straight, and said, "That would be great, Russ. Let me get to the store at the corner and see what I can get my hands on food-wise. Come over when you get a minute. I'd really appreciate it. Thank you, for everything you've told me, and the instructions you gave. I know you think I'm just a pompous asshole, but I grew up dirt poor, and I actually have a good bit of non-perishable food at the house. When you've gone hungry, you don't forget that, and you make sure it doesn't happen again. I'll buy up whatever else I can, but if I can't, I'll still be good for a while. Since I love shooting, I have a few guns, and a few hundred rounds of ammo. I may be able to hold off the scumbags if they show up. I'll go down fighting, that's for damn sure. If you can help me with the stove and a toilet, I think I can handle the rest."

Holy cow. I was stunned at his statements; I knew we all were. We did think he was a shallow, pompous asshole—he'd forgotten the shallow part. Now, we had a whole new view of Brian. Hell, he could be one of us, with a little work. We'd keep that in mind. Another mouth to feed, yes, but another defender as well? That could not be brushed aside. There is strength in numbers, and that was going to be even more true in the coming days, and after.

Brian thanked us again, apologized for taking up our time, and headed back to his house. I may have imagined it, but it looked like he was walking with a purpose. I was very proud of Russ. He could have blown Brian off and sent him on his way, but he had tried to help him in the only way he had at the time—information. Instructions. It was the best we could offer for now. I hoped it would be enough for Brian to survive.

Janet had come back down by now—we had some time while the water bladders filled—and as Russ closed the door, he turned to us with a look of determination. "We've got work to do, and we need to talk. I thought about something while I was talking to Brian. I think we need to bring Bob, Janet, and Ben here. I think we should all be together in one place—we can protect one house better than two. We have a few more amenities here, and an extra bedroom and bath. If you guys are cool with that, we need to get busy moving them and their stuff here. What do you guys think?"

Bob was nodding slowly. Janet had a distinct look of disappointment, which I completely understood. No woman wants to leave her home, her stuff, her kitchen. I would have felt the same way if the shoe had been on the other foot. Ben and Rusty were happy as could be. Roommates! Bob looked at Janet. As much as she hated it, she knew Russ was right. We had more room, we had the chickens and rabbits inside a privacy fence they didn't have. She forced a smile, nodded at her husband, and hugged me. She looked at Russ and said, "Good idea. Where do we start?"

# Chapter 3

It took the better part of the morning to get the supplies from Bob and Janet's place back to ours. As I said, their preps were as deep as ours, and we had all of Bob's protected electronics as well. When we were done, we had completely filled the prep room, with nothing more than a path left through it for now. We'd have time to organize after we'd locked the place down. We couldn't move Bob's garage Faraday cabinet, so we just had to hope and pray there would be no subsequent events. We grabbed clothes, shoes, linens, and some cooking implements I didn't have. We didn't leave a crumb of food or a bottle of water. If some shit heels broke in looking for it, they were going to be disappointed. And probably pissed off. We did fill both tubs with waterBOBs. The shit heels could get water if they got to it before us. We probably wouldn't come back for it, but it was nice to know there were a couple hundred gallons of water over there if we needed it.

Between the two families, now one, we had enough water to take care of us for six months to a year, much longer than that food-wise. If it came down to it, we could stretch that further with the chickens and rabbits in the backyard. Our long-term plan did not require us to make it that long here. We only needed to bug in until the insanity that was coming peaked and started to calm back down. We had prepped for longer in case we couldn't make that happen, for whatever reason.

I have always been a glass-is-half-full kind of gal, so I still held out hope that mankind would rise up and stand together in this crisis. Russ was the opposite, and expected the worst out of people, especially during a crisis. I pointed out how the country had come together after 9/11, and all the people who traveled to New Orleans after Katrina from all over the country to help, including donations of food, water, clothes—that was the America I was confident could survive a TEOTWAWKI—The End Of The World As We Know It—scenario. But Russ woke me from that dream.

"Anne—9/11, Katrina? Those were localized to a small section of the country. How loving and caring do you think those people will be when everybody is in the same boat? Nobody is going to be helping anybody else, because everybody—*everybody*—will be trying to survive themselves. It will be every man for himself. What would you do to protect and feed Rusty? Anything, right? Try to imagine millions of people in the same situation. Now, imagine how many of those people are in any way prepared for something like that to happen. My guess is less than three percent of the population. That means ninety-seven percent are now looters, marauders, raiders, murderers, every slime bag imaginable, trying to survive off what they can get their hands on from robbing and killing those who have something. It's going to be bad, it's going to be ugly, and I want us to be as far from other people as we can get if and when it happens."

As much as I hated to admit it, I could totally see his point. Mankind was only generous when it didn't cost them much of anything to be so. When it came down to survival, we were all capable of things we would never consider doing in "polite" society. I would stand up to anyone who tried to hurt my family, and I wouldn't think twice about using deadly force to do it. I didn't know if I could kill someone to feed my son, but I also couldn't completely rule that out. Anything is possible when you are talking about protecting and feeding your child.

As our plan had always been to go out to the farm for the long haul, we would stay put as long as we felt we could do it without dealing with hordes of starving, desperate people. If what Russ had told Brian was true, we had two to four weeks we could stay where we were. After that, the survivors would be working their way out of town and the burbs, and heading our way. We intended to be gone by then. In case we were mistaken about the timeline and got caught up in any bad situations, we had done some reinforcing around the house.

Russ had replaced all the screws in the deadbolt strike plates. The ones that had come with them were no more than an inch long; he removed them and replaced them with three-inch screws. The logic was sound: a three-inch screw was in the stud, not just the door frame, so we were pretty much assured no one was going to kick in those doors at the deadbolt.

I had seen a picture on a decorating website of what looked like barn doors in rails as a window covering. While the poster labeled it as "country charm," I saw inside shutters that could be bolted shut. Russ had installed them over the big picture window in the living room. To visitors it was quaint; to us, it was reinforcements for a weak defense point. There was some ammo out there that could easily pierce the window glass and shutter, but most people only bought what was considered target ammo. We were gambling that any shooters would have used up the personal defense rounds in town, and would be down to the FMJ—full-metal jacket—target bullets. We hoped we wouldn't have to find out.

That left regular single windows for the rest of the downstairs. Russ had sheets of plywood in the garage ready to go up quickly, with pre-drilled holes for the screws he would use to attach them to the wall. Using the three-inch screws again, he was relatively confident they would hold up to some level of forced entry. We hadn't planned much for upstairs, because if we were forced to run up there by intruders, we were pretty much done. Russ had installed a doorway at the top of the stairs, which would give us a bit of a cushion if all else failed.

We didn't put up the plywood yet; the windows were a source of natural light during the day, which kept us from burning the kerosene lamps or candles. Upside was we could attach them to the walls quickly. The guys brought them in and had them sitting against the walls by each window, ready to go.

With full waterBOBs in both bathtubs, we would be forced to shower in the half-bath, as long as the water held out. Once that was gone, we had an outside shower rigged with a sun shower setup. Basically, a sun shower is a black bag you fill with water and set in the sun, and you let the sun heat the water in the bag. You hang it up and let gravity do the rest. Very rustic, but beggars can't be choosers, and a little shower is better than no shower. We had a couple, as did Bob and Janet, so we should be able to keep enough water hot for short rinses.

The water in the waterBOBs was to be used for drinking and cooking. We had rain barrels outside under every gutter down-spout, so we had a few hundred gallons there we could use for flushing toilets, and possibly washing clothes. We couldn't drink what came off the roof, because of pollution, bird droppings, and pieces of asphalt from the shingles, unless it was a completely dire emergency. Even then, it would have to be filtered and boiled—and I still wasn't sure I could get past bird poop in the water. We did have a two-hundred-gallon cistern sitting in the corner of the backyard to catch rainwater for the livestock and the small garden. We could use that for drinking and cooking if we boiled it first. We had twenty seven-gallon water jugs between us full of water. Each one would provide enough water for one person for a week, for drinking and cooking. That gave us about three and a half weeks of water for six people, if we had to stretch it, not counting the two hundred gallons in the tubs. Altogether, we felt pretty confident about our water stores. Water was the number one, most important thing to have planned out.

Food was the next item of importance. Between us, we had enough food to last us a year, possibly eighteen months, without having to butcher the chickens and rabbits. That seemed like a lot, if we weren't planning to stay that long, but any we hadn't used by the time we headed to the farm would be going with us. Russ had a big box trailer out back, which had been fitted with shelving and strapping. Bob had one as well, along with an old Chevy Blazer that was pre-1980. Both of those were brought over and put in the backyard. For now, we would eat what was going to spoil first, emptying the freezers from both houses. Russ brought out the big generator, fired it up, and set it on the patio outside the sunroom in the backyard. We had bought the quietest one we could find, but none of them are silent. We figured now was the best time to use it, since everyone who might hear it would just be wishing they had one, rather than trying to take it. We pulled out all the dehydrators. None of them had chips in them, thank goodness, so they were still working. We sliced up the beef, venison, and pork that we had as roasts or loins as they thawed. We started making jerky out of everything we thought we'd lose without power. Russ wanted us to be done with it by the end of the third day. It would be close, but we were pretty sure we could meet that deadline.

"Why three days, Dad? What's the deal?" Rusty asked while he was getting the smoker ready for a pork butt and a venison shoulder. Smoked meat lasted longer too.

Russ looked at his son with a sad smile. "Rusty, have you heard of the rule of threes?" Rusty shook his head. Russ continued. "The rule of threes is this: you can last three minutes without air; three days without water; three weeks without food. In three days, people will likely be out of food and water. Most people don't have enough food in their house to last a week. The grocery store only has enough food on the shelves for about seventy-two hours' worth to feed the immediate surrounding community. And there won't be any trucks bringing any more. In three days, people will start leaving their homes, looking for food sources. They will have figured out the government is not coming to rescue them, or at least that it's going to take longer than they first thought. They will start to get desperate to find food and water for themselves and their families. We don't have a lot of neighbors out here, but that doesn't make us safe. The scent of food cooking carries a long way when there are no other smells filling the air, like exhaust. People will follow their noses, especially if they are already hungry. We don't want to lead them here. Understand?"

Rusty looked at his dad and nodded. "What do we do if they come here anyway, Dad? What if they try to take our food and water?" There was a slight quiver to his voice, though he was trying hard to hide it.

Russ looked him in the eye and said, "We stop them, son. We have to stop them. This is our food and water, our supplies. We bought them, we stored them, we planned for something like this. It is not our fault if they didn't, and it is not our responsibility to take care of them now. The people in this house, and Monroe and Millie, are the only ones we are taking care of now. If that sounds harsh, or greedy, or inhumane, it is what it is. I'm not sorry for feeling this way. This is it. Everything you have known in life is changing, right now, in ways you can't imagine yet. We have to be willing to do whatever is necessary to survive." With that said, Russ fired up the smoker and put the meat on to cure.

****

Russ looked around, smiled, and said, "Gang, it looks like we are pretty much on the way to completing stage one, which was setting up for round one. Does anybody have any questions?" We all looked at each other, shook our heads, and let a little bit of the tension seep out of our bodies. It was after noon, and I realized we had missed breakfast and lunch. Great wife and mother I was—the first day of the apocalypse, and I was already forgetting to feed the family.

Just as I was heading back into the kitchen to figure out what to fix, I smelled the delicious aroma of chicken. Janet had snuck inside and put on a pot of soup. She was standing at the stove, stirring and tasting, like any cook worth her salt. She looked at me with a big grin and said, "I found this chicken in the freezer, along with some veggies and noodles. You said pull it and cook it, so lunch is ready!"

I called the guys in, and they all headed for the table. Like a traffic cop, I stood in the way, one hand on my hip, the other held up in a "stop right there" motion. "Ok, gentlemen, let's get one thing straight right now. *Nobody* eats without washing his hands. For that matter, let me give you a quick rundown of the new sanitation rules. Wash your hands *every time* you go to the bathroom. I don't care why you went, wash. At the very least, if you only peed, use the anti-bacterial gel. The other, wash your hands, with soap. No exceptions. If you touch anything outside the house, wash before you come in. There are not going to be any minor emergency clinics, or doctors' offices, or hospitals we can count on, so we have to be diligent in keeping things as clean as we can. In emergency situations, as many people die from disease as anything else. We're going to set up a wash tub on the patio with a pitcher of clean water this afternoon, but for now, we still have water coming from the faucets, so march." Man, I was Betty Bad Ass. Cool.

Russ grinned, the one that said, "That's *my* bitch." He walked into the kitchen, smacked me on the ass, and kissed me on the cheek. He looked at Rusty and Ben, and said, "Mom's right. Let's get washed up." They headed to the sink, while Janet covered her mouth to hide the laughter. We got some food in us, and I for one felt much more energetic for it. We talked while we ate about what else we needed to get done.

Russ looked around with a satisfied smile. "I think we can slow down a little for now. We've gotten pretty much all the preliminary chores done. I'd say take it a little easier for the rest of the day. We are going to need to get a good night's sleep, because after tonight, we will be posting a watch around the clock. The longer this situation goes on, the worse things will get. We need to be ready for whatever may come." Nice, Russ. Way to bring us down off our food high. But he was right, and we all knew it.

He looked at Rusty and said, "Son, I'm going over to check on Brian. I want you to come with me. Go out to the shed and grab a five-gallon bucket, and an empty number ten can, with its lid, an empty soup can, and a pair of tin snips. Drop them all in the bucket, get your pistol, and let's go. I want to get back here before dark."

After Rusty had run out and got the things Russ had asked for, he grabbed his nine-millimeter S&W with its paddle holster and followed his dad out the door. Rusty might not have had to go to school that day, but class was about to start.

# Chapter 4

Brian Riggins had grown up dirt poor. His "sperm donor," as he thought of his biological father, had run out on his mom when she was still pregnant with him. His mom had just turned eighteen when she found out she was pregnant. She got WIC and AFDC. She applied for and got all the "government assistance" she could. She didn't work, but always had money for beer and cigarettes. She made sure there was food in the house, but not quite enough for a growing boy. She added another brother and a sister when Brian was a teenager. Brian thought she had figured out she was going to lose her benefits in a few years when he turned eighteen, so she hedged her bets. With twelve years between him and his brother, Brian was not close to his siblings. At fourteen, he got a job bagging groceries at Grand's Market, a small local grocery store. He took his first paycheck and bought a bike to ride back and forth to work. From that point on, he always had a job.

Brian left home when he was seventeen. He graduated early and started taking classes at the local community college. He got a tiny apartment within walking distance of school. He still worked at Grand's and was by then the assistant manager. Mr. Grand had sort of adopted him and was teaching him how a business worked and ran. The Grand family had owned the grocery for fifty years, and Theodore Grand was in his sixties; he had an idea to turn the store over to Brian when he finished college. Brian had other plans.

Growing up with nothing, he wanted everything. The best of everything. He put himself through the University of Tennessee, majoring in business management. He graduated with honors and started his career with a small local bank. Within five years, he was the head of the financial services division of the largest bank in the South. He had completely remade himself, from a white trash boy living in Section 8 housing to a senior executive with a fancy sports car, a big house, and pretty much anything he could want within his grasp.

He played the part of the rich playboy—well, rich to him, and the people he grew up with—but inside he was still the little boy who wasn't sure if there would be food in the house tomorrow. Because of that, he tended to hoard food. Every time he went to the grocery store, he bought peanut butter and tuna, crackers and ramen noodles, instant oatmeal and cans—no, cases—of soups. He didn't worry about water, counting on the utilities to be there, but he had about a half dozen cases of bottled water just the same. He also had a sub-zero refrigerator, with a freezer full of steaks, pork chops, chicken, and an assortment of TV dinners, for those nights he didn't feel like cooking. He had a huge outdoor kitchen set up in his backyard, with a gas grill and fireplace. He loved to cook—well, cook out—but didn't go out much. For all his brash, asshole attitude, he was very much a loner. He dated rarely and never brought them home. Now, just reaching thirty, he still had no one special in his life. He liked the solitude of his home, because he didn't have to share it with anyone.

If what Russ had said was right, life was about to get interesting. Like, scary interesting. Brian went home, changed into jeans, a sweatshirt, and running shoes, grabbed all his stash cash—about five hundred dollars, another hold over from his childhood—and put his Springfield XDS .40 in his waistband. He grabbed the biggest backpack he owned and pulled his bike down out of the garage. He had always had a bike to ride, ever since that first one, and that was now turning out to be a really good thing. He checked the chain, tested the brakes and gear shift, and deemed it roadworthy.

There was a strip mall right before the on ramp to the interstate, about five miles away; he could get there in about fifteen to twenty minutes. There was something he wanted to buy besides the food Russ had suggested, and he needed to get going right away, before someone else decided they wanted one too.

****

From the time he left their dead-end little road, there were cars sitting here and there along the way. The closer he got to the mall, the more cars he saw—some abandoned, some with the occupants still in or around them. Everyone was milling around, holding their cell phones up like they were looking for service—really? The phone is a brick, and you think raising it in the air will fix that?—but they all had one thing in common: they had no idea what had happened. If they did, they would not be standing around looking for a cell signal. They would be heading home as fast as possible to make sure their families were safe. He thanked whatever powers that be that Russ had leveled with him on what was going on. He felt like he had a leg up on a bunch of other people.

On the other side of the road was a school bus, about half full of kids, mostly teenagers, that would have been headed down his street for the neighbors' kids, then on to the high school. While Brian was on a mission, he felt bad for the children and their parents. He rode over to the other side of the road and up to the bus. The driver had the door open, so Brian went over to it. He looked in to the driver. "Hey, man, you need to get these kids off the bus and have them start walking home."

The driver looked at him, confused, but didn't argue. "You know, I think you're right. I don't know what's going on, but this is just weird." He turned around and made an announcement: "Kids, school's out today. The bus is hosed, so you better get out and try to make your way home. Team up with someone who lives close to you. Hurry." The kids started off the bus, confused, but happy that school was out for the day.

Brian got back on his way to the mall. He got a few strange looks from people still standing by their cars, like they were going to magically come back on. He arrived a few minutes later, and it wasn't crazy there—yet—so he headed to the bike store. This was the first, and most important, stop he had to make.

The store, Riding My Life Away, was open but dark. He had bought the bike he was riding there, and the owner, Mitch, was at the door.

"Hey, Brian. Strange day, huh? We're open, but no power, so no credit card purchases. Cash still works, and checks. What are you looking for?"

Brian walked his bike in, beckoned Mitch to follow him, and shut the door. Mitch gave him a curious look but did as he was asked. Brian gave him the highlights of Russ's theory of what had happened. Mitch listened, wide-eyed and somewhat skeptical, but he was a smart guy, and Brian knew he would see the common sense in the theory.

Mitch looked at Brian and said, "I need to head home. What do you need? Let's do this quick, so I can get out of here. I hope you have cash."

Brian smiled and pulled out his wad of cash. He wouldn't have done that in front of just anybody, but he trusted Mitch.

Brian pointed to the covered trailers stacked in the corner. "I want to buy one of those bike trailers up there. Will two hundred dollars cash take care of it?" Mitch looked over at the trailers. The price tag said $199.

"Hell yes. In fact, we're having a shit-hit-the-fan sale—fifty percent off all trailers. A hundred dollars, tax included. Cash only. All sales are final." Mitch had a smirky grin on his face as he grabbed one of the trailers for Brian, and one for himself. Brian handed him a hundred-dollar bill, shook his hand, and hooked the trailer to his bike.

"Thanks, Mitch. Do yourself a favor—lock this place up, head to the grocery store with all the cash you have, load up, head home, and lock down. It's probably going to get ugly fast. The closer you live to town, the quicker the bad will show up. Good luck. We're all going to need it." Mitch shook his hand again, and Brian headed across the parking lot to the grocery store.

The store was open, surprisingly. The manager was at the door, greeting incoming customers with a rehearsed litany: "Good morning. We are experiencing some power issues, so we are not able to accept credit card payments. Cash and personal checks are fine. It's a bit dark, but the skylights will help. Let me know if I can be of any assistance."

Brian rode up and smiled at the manager. "Good morning. Okay if I bring my bike in? I don't want to leave it outside with everything all weird out here."

The manager, looking confused but not wanting to lose a customer, smiled and said, "Of course. Come on in."

Brian started with the bottled water. He loaded up six cases, so as not to raise a lot of suspicion, but enough to carry him for a few weeks. He grabbed some coffee, tea, instant drink mixes, dry milk, sugar, and flour. Then he went to the canned goods and got a variety of pastas, soups, tuna, and chicken. Next, he went to the cracker and cookie aisle and grabbed a dozen each of multiple brands and types. Finally, he grabbed a couple of loaves of bread, as well as some bagels and English muffins. Those would last a couple of weeks longer than the bread, if not more. In all, he had a little over a hundred dollars in food and water. He headed to the cashier. Surprisingly, there were only a few people in the store, but some of them were buying the same types of items Brian was. When he happened to make eye contact with one man, he responded with a slight nod, and moved on. They knew. They knew he knew. He silently thanked Russ again for what he had done for him, telling him what was happening, opening his eyes to the truth.

At the register, the cashier looked at the pile in the bike cart and then at the manager. He came over, looked in the cart, then said to Brian, "Sir, do you have any idea how much all of that is? We don't have access to the computer system, so we don't know any of the prices without going and looking them all up. Let me see what we can do …" He looked a little lost.

Brian took charge. He looked at the man's name tag. "Will? My name is Brian. I believe this adds up to about a hundred dollars before tax, but just to be safe, and make sure you are covered, I'm going to give you a hundred and fifty, along with my name, address, and phone number. If you come up short, when the power comes back on, you let me know, and I'll help you cover it." Brian knew he wouldn't have to fulfill that commitment. The power wasn't coming back on anytime soon.

Will smiled at him. "I think a hundred and fifty dollars would more than cover it. Thank you for your honesty and integrity, sir. Have a great day!" Brian thanked him and headed out the door. He had one more stop to make before he headed home. He had $250 left and was planning to spend it all in one place.

Outdoor Living was at the end of the strip mall. They had camping gear, but more importantly, hunting gear. He rode his bike to the store; again, it was open. He was saddened by the many people who didn't understand what was happening, and had opened the stores like the power would be on any time. But then, where would he be if Russ hadn't told him what he did? He'd be trying to get to the office, for Pete's sake.

He started to walk his bike in but was stopped by a security guard as soon as he got to the door. "Sir, you can't bring that rig into the store."

Brian stopped. "With all the weird stuff going on this morning, I'm worried someone will grab it. Can I leave it here with you?"

The guard looked him over, and apparently was impressed with the fact he'd asked to leave it with him and hadn't given him any shit. "Sure, man, I'll keep my eye on it for you."

Brian checked his name tag. "I appreciate it, John. I won't be long, I promise." He headed back to the hunting section.

A young associate greeted him with a smile and let him know they could not take credit cards; Brian replied that he would be paying in cash. He bought ammo for his pistols, shotgun, and rifles. He got the least expensive so he could get the highest quantities. He ran his total up to $225. The associate added it up on a piece of paper and told Brian he wouldn't charge him tax, because everything was down. Brian went back and got two more boxes of pistol ammo, to get it closer to $250. He handed over the cash, and when the young man asked if he wanted him to write up a receipt, Brian told him that wouldn't be necessary, to just keep the list for his own records.

He went back to the front, thanked John again for watching his stuff, added his purchases to the trailer, and headed home. He felt like he had done the best he could with the cash he had. On the way back, there were fewer people on the road with their cars. It looked like more of them had decided they needed to try to get home. He hoped they would make it. He knew some might not, due to how far they needed to travel, what they were wearing—he imagined himself in his dress shoes trying to walk five miles, let alone fifteen or twenty—and lack of food and water; the odds were not in the modern man's favor. Oh well, he needed to focus on himself and his own survival.

When he got home, he rode the bike around back and took it in the house through the back door. He unloaded his purchases on the dining room table and looked around his house. Not really built for security. He would need to see what he could do to create at least a secure area inside the house. Maybe Russ would have some ideas; he'd ask when he came over. Right then, there was a knock at the door. Ask, and you shall receive. He smiled at his own humorous thought, and headed to the door.

\*\*\*\*

With Rusty waiting behind him, bucket in hand, Russ knocked on the door; it was just a few moments before Brian opened it. He offered a smile and a handshake. "Hey, Russ. Thank you for coming over. Come in, come in. I know you have a lot to do. Let's get to work."

Russ looked at Brian, both surprised and impressed with the apparent change in his attitude and demeanor. He walked inside and immediately saw a dining room table loaded with goods, and a bike and trailer against the wall. He smiled at Brian and nodded. "You've been busy this morning."

Brian smiled back. "Yeah, I'm really a smart guy. You don't have to smack me upside the head to get my attention." Russ looked through the items on the table with a new respect for their owner. Maybe they had been wrong about Brian. If he'd picked up on the situation that fast, he could become an ally in things going forward.

"Brian, I have to tell you, I am beyond impressed with your comprehension of this whole new world. I need to talk to the others, but if they are in agreement, I think we should consider an alliance. No one will be able to make it alone once things start to get really ugly, and I believe we could help each other. In the meantime, let's make sure you can cook food and safely dispose of the aftermath." Russ laughed at his own attempt at a clean joke, and Brian grimaced but joined in the fun.

Rusty set the bucket down, and Russ started unloading it. He pulled out the cans first, then grabbed the tin snips and looked up at Brian. "Do you have a marker?"

"Sure, let me grab one." Brian rummaged through one of the kitchen drawers and pulled out a fine-tipped permanent marker. "Will this work?"

Russ took the pen, gave it the once over, and nodded. "Perfect. Rusty, hand me the soup can." Rusty was still in the dark as to what they were going to do. He handed his dad the can, and Russ took it and held it up against the side of the number ten can close to the bottom, drew an outline of the soup can against the larger one, and set both aside. He picked up the snips and addressed his captive audience.

"We're building a rocket stove. The premise behind the design is you get a lot of heat for a little bit of fuel. Especially for one person, this is a great design for cooking food and boiling water for purification. First, you take a number ten can—the size you find in the bulk section of the grocery store. Then, take a soup can, or any regular-sized vegetable can, and cut a hole in the big one the size of the smaller one. The cylindrical design channels the heat created by the fuel—in this case, sticks you find in the yard. Rusty, go out back and pick up any twigs you see." Rusty went out the back door while Russ continued his work on the stove. Brian was watching with rapt attention.

Russ cut the hole in the larger can and inserted the smaller one. "We could get more efficiency if we had a shelf for the fuel source, but this will serve the purpose for now."

Rusty came back in with a handful of twigs and handed them to his dad. Russ laid them beside the stove and looked at Brian again. "Paper? Lighter? Matches?"

Brian went back to his drawer and pulled out a lighter and a few books of bar matches. He handed them all to Russ; Russ took one book of matches and handed the rest back to Brian. "Put these someplace you can find them quick. Hand me that pad of Post-it notes." Russ took a few notes, crumpled them into little balls, and pushed them inside the smaller can. He lit a match and touched it to the closest paper ball, which caught fire quickly. Russ put some of the smallest twigs in with the burning paper; they lit almost immediately.

"Wow, Russ," Brian said. He sounded impressed. "That's awesome. I can't believe how fast that started. How long will it burn?"

Russ stood up, looked at Brian, and smiled a very self-satisfied smile. "As long as you feed it. Hold your hand over the top of the big can. Feel that heat?"

Brian did as he was instructed and quickly pulled his hand back. "Oh, man. That is super hot. I'm pretty sure I can cook some ramen noodles on that bad boy. I have a small charcoal grill under the house. I bet I can use the grate from that grill on this and get a stable platform. Thank you for this. I'm going to start by cooking the meat in the freezer tomorrow. I think it will be okay until then."

Russ nodded his agreement. "Yes, if you keep the freezer door shut it will be fine until tomorrow, probably longer. Okay, next up, porta-potty." He grabbed the five-gallon bucket and handed it to Brian. "You're going to need another bucket, or a can, to save your ashes in from the rocket stove. Do you have something?"

Brian went out to the garage, and a minute later was back with a metal ash bucket. Russ nodded his approval. "Perfect. Whenever you aren't using the stove, dump the ashes in that bucket. The big plastic bucket will be your toilet. You can actually remove one of your toilet seats and place it on the bucket for a more comfortable feeling. When you use the potty, dump some of the ashes on the top—it will help cut down the smell. That's about the best you can do, short term. Of course, you should use your toilet as long as it flushes. This is for after that service stops."

Russ looked at the items on the dining table again. "You did really well, Brian. I misjudged you. I'm sorry. We need to talk again, maybe tomorrow. Does that work for you?"

Brian smiled. "Sure, Russ. Come by any time. It's not like I have to get to work or anything." They both laughed at the joke.

Russ got serious again. "What I said before, about not coming back to the house—come over if you need anything. We'll talk again soon." Russ called Rusty over; they both shook Brian's hand, then headed back home. Brian had a pretty good setup for now. Russ had no doubt he'd be back to talk to him in the next day or so. Without even trying, Brian had transformed himself from an annoyance to a possible ally.

By the time they got back, it was getting dark; there were emergency lanterns burning in the house. After a dinner of warmed-over chicken soup and some homemade cornbread, everyone was pretty wiped out. Russ made sure everyone had a place to pass out, and then they promptly did. The next day, there was more work to be done. A lot more.

# Chapter 5

The next morning, we awoke to differing levels of restfulness. The boys were fine. They could sleep through anything, no matter the circumstances. The guys were a bit less fully rested, but had still slept well. They didn't know why they hadn't gotten a good night's sleep, but they were no worse for the wear.

Janet and I were the most affected. I can only guess it was the "mom hearing." Janet agreed. "I woke up all night long, because there wasn't any noise. That sounds stupid, I know, but I think I'm used to fans and electric motors running in the background of life. I know I'll get used to it, but right now, I miss the hum of electricity in the world." She had nailed it. It was the lack of background noise that had woken me more than once in the night. I knew I'd get used to it as well as Janet, I just wondered how long it would take. No fan while I was sleeping? That really sucked.

We made coffee on the camp stove in the sunroom, then fresh eggs from the chickens and bacon thawing from the freezer. Might as well cook it if we had it, because we wouldn't have it for long. Janet topped off the awesome breakfast with biscuits cooked in an oven that worked off the heat of a camp stove, the same method she had used for the cornbread the night before. Between the two families, we had four stoves, with probably three dozen bottles of propane, so we had plenty of options for cooking.

As we were eating a family breakfast, with everyone there, Russ said we needed to talk about Brian. Bob laughed. "Dude, we have a lot more interesting, and much more important, things to talk about than that douche. I figured after you went over there yesterday, you finalized our dealings with him. What now?"

Russ smiled and proceeded to tell us about everything Brian had done after coming over the morning before. To say we were as impressed as Russ was putting it mildly. We had all thought he was a shallow, self-serving rich boy, who would be one of the first to go down in a situation like the one we were currently facing. Russ went on to fill us in on his idea.

"As things degrade, there will be more and more troubles headed our way. You can never have too many people when it comes to security. I think we should offer to bring him in here, and when we head to the farm, see if he wants to come along. He is smart and savvy when it comes to surviving. I don't know what in his past made him this way, but he could definitely be an asset, now and in the future. When we get to the farm, there will be a lot more to secure, and we will need more bodies. I think we should feel him out, and if he doesn't have any family or a fallback location, we can offer him a place with us. I'm ready to debate this if we need to." Russ looked around the table at each of us.

As his wife, and after what he had gone through to open my eyes to prepping, I didn't doubt Russ anymore. If he said Brian was a good guy and would be an asset, I was in. Bob and Janet would be the voters. Janet would go along with Bob, or me, for that matter, so it really came down to Bob.

He looked at Russ, clearly surprised. "Brother, if you think we need him, we need him. I wouldn't have believed it if it came from anyone other than you. That just leaves one question: is he bunking in with you and Anne, or me and Janet? We could make him a pallet on the floor with the boys."

He grinned at Russ, and we all laughed. "No, I think we can set him up in the den, at least until things start to get really ugly. I think we should invite him to dinner this evening. Can we cook a dinner that's guest-worthy tonight?"

Janet and I both smiled and nodded. "I'm sure we can come up with something enticing. Lord knows, we still have freezer food thawing as we speak. Leave that to us." I held up my hand for the high five that Janet returned while the guys laughed again.

"Good deal. Bob and I will go over this afternoon and invite him for dinner. I think you will all be pleasantly surprised at who he really is. Until then, we have some stuff to work on. Boys, eat up. We have work to do." The boys shoved the last bites of eggs and biscuits in their mouths, downed their orange juice—more frozen stuff thawing—and put their shoes on. As they were all heading out the door, I held up my hand in that traffic cop stance again. Maybe I had missed my calling.

"Attention! Dental hygiene alert! In case you hadn't considered it, there won't be a lot of dentists in business for a while. Until further notice, everyone will brush and floss after every meal. We can't afford to get cavities, and there won't be any root canals being done. Go brush and floss, everybody." It's the little things that can cause the biggest problems.

They all headed to the bathrooms to do as they were bid. As I was contemplating the lack of doctors and dentists, it dawned on me that I hadn't even thought about my job, or my boss. I worked as a bookkeeper for a restaurant equipment company. My boss was an alright guy, but he had given me a rash of shit for being a prepper. Not that I had let him know how in-depth our prepping actually went, but he had seen my GHB in my SUV and asked what it was. When I told him, he laughed for five minutes.

"Anne, are you kidding me? A woman as smart as you worrying about something as unlikely as that?"

I wondered how he felt about all that now. I said a quick prayer for him and his family and then moved on. When the SHTF, my family came first. As the guys came back down the hall, I headed back to obey my own dental hygiene edict. I had a feeling it was going to be a busy day.

****

Russ took Bob and the boys out to the backyard. It was early spring in Tennessee, so the temps were mild, thankfully. Come the summer, if the power was still out, we were going to find out firsthand what our grandparents' lives had been like before air conditioning. Did I mention how much no electricity sucks?

Glancing out the glass doors, I saw they had gone to the storage building and were organizing the piles we had dumped there from what we had grabbed at Bob and Janet's. Russ opened the first trailer, pulled out the ramp, and walked in. He turned on a light and scooted some boxes against the wall.

"Alright, fellas, we need to get these piles organized. I want us to be ready to go as fast as possible, in case everything turns to shit. Heavy stuff goes on the bottom, but don't fill the floor up. We need to save room for last-minute items that might be heavy or cumbersome. Oh, and watch out for the garden. If you step on those plants, you are toast. You know how your mom loves radishes."

We had turned up a small plot for a garden. We would get plenty of fresh veggies from the farm during the summer, but it was also nice to have some right out back—tomatoes, cucumbers, radishes, and best of all, lettuce—those things we could eat every day, and did. The radishes were almost ready, and the lettuce was ripe enough to start pulling, but the tomato and cucumber sets were still in the sunroom. No reason to plant them now. I'd just keep them watered, and hope we could take them with us to the farm. Not that Millie wouldn't have some as well, but they were already started. And can you ever really have too many tomatoes or cucumbers?

I was watching the guys out the back door when Janet walked in from the garage carrying a half-thawed roast. "Do you think Russ would fire the generator up again, so we can use the slow cooker? If not, I'm going to have to try to cook this on the camp stove, and I've never cooked a roast that way. If we can use the slow cooker, we can set it and forget it. Come to think of it, do we even know if the slow cooker still works?"

I shrugged and headed for the pantry. "No idea, but there's only one way to find out." I pulled out the cooker and crossed my fingers.

Janet went to the door and called out, "Russ, can we get power to run an outlet for the slow cooker? We want to make a roast for dinner tonight. That should be company worthy."

I heard Russ yelling back. "I can do you one better than that. I have a little gem that should work for you. Let me get it."

A few minutes later he came inside carrying a small portable power pack. "This is one of my must-haves from the Faraday cage. I just refreshed the charge on this last weekend. I think the battery will last through your cook time."

He carried the pack into the kitchen and set it on the counter. He turned it on, and showed Janet where to plug the cooker into it.

She quickly put the roast and seasonings together, put the lid on, and turned on the power. The light lit on the front, and we cheered. No chip then. Sweet! I went up to Russ, planted a big kiss on him, and shooed him back out the door.

We still got Russ to fire up the generator, since we were still working on dehydrating meat. He thought we would be safe to use it for the day; the next day was another story, but we were ahead of schedule and almost done, so we should be able to get it done in time.

After a lunch of fried pork chops and French fries—yes, I know, not so healthy, but the freezer was still thawing stuff faster than we could cook it—Russ and Bob headed over to Brian's house. The guys had spent a very productive morning getting the supplies and trailers organized, so Russ had the boys splitting wood. We had a wood-burning stove in the den, and though he didn't think we would run out of propane for the camp stoves, better safe than sorry. If we had to, we could cook on the wood stove. Plus, keeping them busy kept their minds off all the technology they no longer had. Both boys were huge gamers, playing pretty much every night and on weekends, and a lot of the time past their gaming curfews. More importantly, tired kids went to sleep quickly and slept soundly. I was willing to bet they would crash right after supper that night.

Janet and I had been working on the dehydrated foods, packing them in food storage bags. The vacuum sealer apparently had a chip, because it was dead, so we were using zipper bags and a straw. We put the food in, slid the straw to the end, zipped the bag closed to the straw, sucked out the air, pulled the straw, and quickly finished closing the bag. It didn't seal them completely, but close enough to keep the food edible for quite a while.

We finished up the packaging and set a pot of coffee to brewing on the camp stove. We thought the guys would like a cup when they got back, and we definitely were ready for one. We had many pounds of coffee stored, as well as teas, and hot cocoa mix for the boys; when we were gathering our preps, we had tried to think of things we'd miss the most, and coffee was definitely one of them.

We didn't know how long it would be until factories started back up, or when deliveries would begin again, or even if either of those things *would* happen again, ever. We had been firing up the handheld ham radio, but so far had gotten nothing but static. If we weren't even picking up people in other cities, this event was very widespread—possibly impacting the whole country, maybe the world. With no technology, there was no communication, so we were literally in the dark. No matter how much we thought we had prepared for something like this, who knew how vast this was, or how long it would last? We hadn't seen or heard from another soul since it happened. We lived at the end of a short dead-end road, so we didn't get a lot of traffic, but none of the other half dozen neighbors had made it back from wherever they were when the lights went out. That didn't bode well for society or the future.

And just as I was pondering the fact that we hadn't heard another vehicle since the morning before, the unmistakable sound of a loud exhaust came from outside. We quickly killed the generator, closed the shutters over the picture window, and looked through the crack to the street. An old truck, driving down our dead-end street. Trouble. No doubt.

****

"Man, I hope you know what you're doing. I mean, he seems like such a douche." Bob looked at Russ as they walked across the yard toward Brian's house.

Russ smiled at his best friend. "I know. I felt the same way when I opened the door and saw him on the porch yesterday. But I'm telling you, whether he realizes it or not, he has prepper in him. And we will need as many like-minded people as we can find to keep everyone safe."

"Okay, buddy, but if he goes to the douche side, he's gotta go." Russ laughed and stepped up on the porch at Brian's house. He knocked on the door. After a moment, about the time it would have taken Brian to walk from the back of the house to the door and look through the peephole, the door opened.

Brian smiled at them, and they both shook hands with him. "Come in, guys. Can I get you anything? Water, or water?" Russ grinned and declined. They went to the kitchen and sat at the breakfast bar. Russ looked around and saw that all the supplies that had been on the table the day before were gone, apparently stored out of sight of any prying eyes. Good job, Brian.

Russ started the conversation. "Brian, you probably figured out yesterday after we talked that we have an idea what happened. We are what you might have heard referred to as preppers. We have supplies to last without going to stores, and if necessary without services. Have you heard of this kind of lifestyle?"

Brian looked from Russ to Bob and nodded. "Yes, I've heard of it. I don't know that I truly bought into the thought process, but now, it all makes sense. You guys should be in a great position to deal with this. I wish I had gone down that path. I bet there are a lot of people out there now that are wishing the same thing. I really appreciate what you did yesterday, Russ. I was able to get supplies that may help me make it a while, as long as no assholes show up trying to take my stuff. If they do, they'll get a little surprise. I won't give up without a fight."

Russ looked at Bob, who was grinning like a Cheshire cat. Bob took over the chat. "We have a proposition for you, Brian. You know there is strength in numbers. We have six people at Russ's who can defend what we have. I don't know what all you have, but you won't last long by yourself. We want to invite you to join us over there. It won't be private—you'll probably have to sleep on the couch—but we can offer you friendship, security, and some pretty decent cooking from our wives. In fact, we want you to come over for dinner tonight and get to know everybody a little better. Would you be interested? I think there's a roast cooking as we speak."

Brian smiled at Bob, then Russ. "That sounds great, guys, and the offer to join you sounds even better. I know I've been a dick …" He paused, like he was expecting one of them to disagree with him. They didn't. He laughed and continued. "But I think I could bring something to the table, and I would definitely be in your debt. What time is dinner?"

Russ looked at his arm, where he wasn't wearing a watch anymore. "I don't know about yours, but none of my watches work now. If you want to change clothes, you can come over when you get ready, or if you want, you can come back with us now. We'll probably be eating in a couple of hours. We can talk more while we wait."

Brian stood up, grabbing a .40 and sliding it in his waistband, then crossed to the front door. "I love roast. Let's go. Wait, let me grab something to bring to dinner." He went to a closet off the kitchen, opened the door, and pulled out two bottles of wine. He turned and looked at the guys, a question in his eyes. "Yes? You guys aren't anti-alcohol, are you?"

Bob looked at the wine. "I prefer a good bourbon, but this will go much better with dinner. We'll get to the bourbon later." He reached for one of the bottles and went toward the door. Russ and Brian laughed and followed him.

Bob grabbed the doorknob, and froze. They all heard it; was that a car, running?

\*\*\*\*

Janet and I ran to the window and looked out front. An old pickup, like '75 or so, was coming down the street. The boys came running in from the backyard.

"Mom! I hear a truck or something!" Rusty was so excited, probably at the thought there were other living people besides us. Unfortunately for him, we weren't going to be inviting them in for coffee. If Russ hadn't taught me anything else, it was that once something catastrophic happened, we couldn't trust people blindly anymore.

"Rusty, Ben, you boys get upstairs. Grab your pistols, shut the door, and don't come back down until we call you." Rusty grumbled, but they headed for the stairs. "Go ahead and get cleaned up while you're up there. Dinner is soon, if this isn't trouble. I mean it, stay up there until we tell you to come down."

The boys had no sooner closed the door at the top of the stairs than Russ and Bob came bursting through the back door. They had Brian with them, and a couple of bottles of wine. I'm sure there was a reason for that, but finding out what it was would wait. I was surprised at them coming in the back, and I'm sure my face showed it.

Russ was headed for the front window, but said over his shoulder, "We heard the truck, used a ladder from Brian's place, and came over the fence. We didn't want anyone to see us. Have you seen anybody—has anyone gotten out of the truck?" At the window, he pulled the barn door shutters tighter together, then looked through the crack between them at the street.

I joined him and looked over his shoulder. "No, we haven't seen any people. When I saw the truck, I closed the shutters and sent the boys upstairs. Can you see anybody out there?"

Russ shook his head. "Hand me the binoculars, babe." I went over to the corner and grabbed Russ's bug out bag. In the front pocket was a small pair of binoculars. I handed them to Russ, and he dialed in the focus and looked outside.

"I see two guys in the cab. The driver is driving real slow, and looking at the houses. The passenger has some kind of shotgun. He isn't pointing it out of the truck, but he does have it ready. It looks like they are looking to see if people are home. They could be planning out places to ransack for supplies. Where are the boys?" He was obviously a little rattled, since I had told him I had sent the boys upstairs. He put his hand on his pistol.

"I sent them upstairs and told them to stay until we called them. Would there be people doing that already? It hasn't even been forty-eight hours since the pulse. I mean, I knew it would happen, but I didn't expect it this fast. What should we do?" I was surprised, and disappointed, because if things had gone to shit this fast, we would have to step up our plans to get to the farm.

Russ put his arms around me and pulled me close. "Right now, we're just going to watch and see what they do. Hopefully, they're just checking for future reference and are going down more streets than this one. Everybody just stay quiet and wait."

We were all by the shutters, looking out at the street. The truck didn't stop, but it did go very slowly down the road to the dead end, then turned around and worked its way back up and out of the neighborhood. We breathed a collective sigh of relief. They were gone for now, but still … Russ looked at us and gave us a half-smile. At least there was part of a smile, so we weren't completely hosed … for now, at least.

"Is dinner ready? We need to talk, all of us. Get the boys, and let's sit down. By the way, Brian brought wine for dinner. I think we'll be needing that." I didn't disagree. None of us did. Things were about to get serious. Dammit.

# Chapter 6

After a wonderful dinner of roast, potatoes, beans, and rolls—I would miss rolls when yeast was gone—and a very nice red wine, we had worked out a plan. We still wanted to stay at the house for as long as possible. For now, we would start security measures and step up the loading of the trailers with what we wanted to take to the farm.

The first couple of weeks would be the most dangerous, once people's food ran out and there was nothing else at the grocery stores. Into the third week, there would start to be die-off of those unable to acquire food and clean water. Unclean water would have taken out the unknowing, the ones who mistakenly drank water that "looked okay." The elderly, the very young, and those hospitalized would have died in the first two weeks. No power to run life support, dialysis, oxygen machines, or anything electronic would show no mercy to those who needed these things to live. Ironically, the deaths of the first ones would increase the danger to the lives of those still here. No services to properly dispose of the bodies meant more diseases for the living. Smart people would at least burn the bodies, but who would take care of the ones in the hospitals and nursing homes? No one was working—they were all trying to survive, looking for supplies to feed their families. The infirm would die quickly as well. Then there was the trash and human waste. People take for granted that these things will be handled by someone in the modern world, and they don't think about how they would do this for themselves if they had to. Now, they had to, but what was more important—burning trash and dead bodies, burying what you used to flush down the toilet, all to ward off diseases that, by the way, there were no doctors or meds to treat if you got them—or finding food and water, so you and your family could survive?

The more time that passed, the fewer people there would be alive in need of resources. But the majority of the ones who survived would very likely be of the non-savory persona. Those survivors would have killed people for their supplies. They would have banded with others like them into gangs, and they would be looking for ways to further their efforts through intimidation and violence. They would take what they wanted, whether it was food or something more sinister. With no police or consequences, criminals of all kinds would be running free, doing whatever they wanted to get whatever they wanted or needed. They would start in the cities, because that's where the largest populations would be, so more possibilities for food, water, weapons—between the stores they could loot, and the people they could take from, they could last there for weeks. But eventually, things would run dry there, and they would have to widen their range for gathering supplies. The suburbs outside the cities would be their next targets, but those places would have little to nothing to offer the gangs, since the people there would have been using those potential resources for their own families. So they wouldn't be in the burbs long. After that, rural areas like ours would hit their radar. We didn't want to be there when that happened.

Russ had relayed all of this to us over dinner. Thankfully, he saved the grossest parts until we had finished eating. Now that he had given us the worst-case scenario, we couldn't sit around and wait for them to get here. "First thing we do is start a twenty-four-hour watch. The visitors we saw today are reason enough. Someone will be awake at all times. Us guys will handle that for now. We can do two- to three-hour watches at night."

I started to protest, but he stopped me. "Anne, I know what you're going to say, but I want you and Janet, and the boys, working on getting the supplies loaded in the trailers. You gals know what food, clothes, linens, first aid, and toiletries we can use, and you pack better than us." He grinned when he said the last part. He was right. We did. We could get more stuff in less space. I think it was a love of puzzles that made us that way.

Bob took over the conversation. "Russ, Brian, and I will work out a schedule for security. I'll step up and offer to take the least-favorite shift from one a.m. to four a.m. Those are the most dangerous hours as far as falling asleep on watch. As long as you gals keep me caffeinated, I'll be good. But I have to fulfill a promise

70

to Brian first. I promised a good bourbon after dinner, and I think we could definitely use it."

He headed to the kitchen, and came back to the table with the Wild Turkey and five glasses. He looked at Rusty and Ben, and motioned to the stairs. "Boys, go play a game or something. We got some grown-up shit to talk about."

The boys snickered but did as they were told. Like they were going to complain about playing a game. They couldn't get online, but they had some pass-and-play games on the mini tablet. They could deal with that.

I looked at Brian. "So, it looks like you'll be joining us. With people roaming the roads, I think we should move you in as soon as possible. You guys need to take wheelbarrows, or whatever we can use, over to Brian's, get his stuff, and get him set up here as soon as possible. Brian, we don't have a spare bedroom, but we'll set you up in the den. There's a hide-a-bed in the sofa, and you can at least close the door. I think we should do this tonight. What can we do to help?"

Russ raised his glass. "I'd like to propose a toast. To our families, and our new addition. May we stay safe until we can get to the farm." We all raised our glasses, and downed the bourbon. That warm sensation went down to my toes.

As we put our glasses on the table, Bob started to refill them, but Russ stayed his hand. "Let's get Brian moved in first, then we can chill a bit more. Brian, are you ready to do this?"

Brian nodded. "With folks already casing the neighborhood? Hell yeah! What's the best way to do this?" We all thought for a moment, then Janet spoke up.

"I think we should do something like a fire brigade, over the fence. We don't want to go through the front yards, in case there are people watching. If we do it out back, the fence should shield most of our activity. Brian can pass to me in his backyard, I can pass to Bob at the fence, Bob can pass to Russ over the fence, Russ can pass to Anne, who can either set it on the patio or in the yard. The boys can help as well. As long as we get it in the backyard here, we can move it later. Would that work?" We all agreed that was an excellent idea. Russ got a ladder from the shed, and we got started.

It took about an hour to get all of Brian's supplies over to our house. He had an impressive amount of food stores for a single guy. I was sure there was a story behind that, but we had plenty of time to hear about it later. He sent his bike and trailer over as well. Who knew if something like that could come in handy in the future? He brought a variety of clothes for all seasons, which told us he didn't intend on going back to his place for a while, if ever. He locked up his house, climbed the ladder to the top of the fence, reached over to his yard and grabbed the ladder, and hauled it up and over to our side.

"Don't want those assholes knowing someone or something is over here." Good thinking, Brian. He continued to amaze me. I couldn't wait to hear his story. Somehow, I had a feeling we were going to have lots of time to talk later.

We all worked together to bring Brian's stuff into the house—to the kitchen, den, or garage, depending on what it was. Once that was done, Russ looked at Brian. "You want first shift or third?"

Brian reached for his pistol. "I'm pretty wired from everything that has happened today. I can take first shift. Can you get to sleep pretty quick?" Russ grabbed the bourbon bottle, turned it up for a good hit, and set it back on the table.

"Yeah, that should help. You wake Bob at one. Bob, you wake me at four. Does anybody have a watch that still works?"

Bob pulled out a wind-up pocket watch. "My grandpa's pocket watch. From old to gold. Grandpa would be so proud. Good thing I've kept it wound." He handed it to Brian. "Get me up at one, buddy. Just knock on the door. I'm a light sleeper."

Brian took the watch and pulled a bar stool up to the front windows. He glanced back at us with a determined look on his face. "Get some rest, gang. This may get really interesting, real soon." He had no idea how right he was, unfortunately. The game was going to change quickly.


\*\*\*\*


73

Fortunately, the night was uneventful. No more drive-bys, all quiet outside. In the morning, Janet and I put on a big pot of coffee, gathered fresh eggs from the chickens, and made omelets with the last of the ham and cheese from the fridge. We had moved everything we could from the fridge to the freezer yesterday, trying to get as much cold as we could from the now-useless appliances. I had frozen water in two-liter soda bottles, rinsed and filled and placed in the bottom of the freezer, for this purpose, as well as emergency drinking water when they thawed. Those bottles were still keeping the inside of the freezer cool enough to act as a cold storage. We might get another day or so of use out of the appliance with this setup, maybe more. We made toast in campfire stands over the camp stoves. With what Brian had brought from his house, we had almost four loaves of bread we needed to use. The one from our place was getting to toast age anyway, because I would have been going to the grocery store in a couple of days. It was weird to think that I wouldn't be grocery shopping again for a while.

I wondered what things were like outside of our little corner of the world. None of us had left the house since it happened, except Brian. It had been over forty-eight hours since everything went down, and I was sure a lot had changed. When I broached the subject at breakfast, Brian spoke up.

"If you want, I can ride my bike out to the main street and take a look around. I'm kind of curious myself."

Russ looked at him and started shaking his head. "I don't know, Brian. It could be getting dicey out there. I also wouldn't want you to go straight out of here, or come straight back, in case anyone was watching. We don't want anyone to know we're here, for as long as possible."

Brian nodded. "I agree, and I actually had a route in mind that would take me through the woods out back. I've ridden there quite a bit, and know my way around. What do you think?"

Russ considered it and stood up. "Yep, I think that might not be such a bad idea, and I think I'll join you. I can ride Rusty's bike. Let me get the boys busy with some chores, and we can head out. Do you have a bug out bag, Brian?"

Brian looked confused. "I might, if I knew what it was."

Russ laughed, along with the rest of us. Next lesson, Brian: prepping 101. Always have a BOB. "It's a backpack that is filled with items you can use to survive if you have to leave home in an emergency situation. You put items in that you think you would need—energy bars, water filter, spare underwear and socks, a way to start a fire, an emergency blanket, a mini first aid kit—the list is long and adaptable to the person. So, you got one?"

Brian looked thoughtful. "No, but I think I can come up with one. Give me a few minutes." Brian disappeared into the den.

While he was gone, Russ called the boys to him. "Okay, fellas, there's chores to do. I want you to check with your moms to see if they need anything done, then go to the preps room and start reorganizing everything we brought over from Bob and Janet's, as well as Brian's stuff. We need to get everything sorted together that is the same, so when we have to start loading the trailers we can keep it all in some kind of order. I also want you to stack the wood you split yesterday. You left a mess out there. Any questions?"

Ben and Rusty looked kind of disappointed. "But Dad, it's not a school day. We have to work all day?"

Russ looked at Rusty with a smirk. "Son, the world you knew before is pretty much gone. There is no screwing around all day on non-school days anymore. Everything is about food and water, heating and cooking, the act of surviving. No, it will not be work all the time, but right now, it is. We have a lot to do to get everything ready to go to the farm. We all have to work on that. Understand?"

Rusty and Ben both nodded and headed for the back door.

I stepped in front of them. "Forgetting something? Brushing? Flossing?" They looked heavenward, which I think they did in an attempt to not roll their eyes in my presence. Good thing, because that would have gotten them a smack. They turned around and headed to the bathroom.

Brian came out of the den with a nice backpack, not one of those cheapies from the dollar store. He showed it to Russ. "This is what I could come up with. Maybe you can help me finish it."

Russ looked inside. "Water, granola bars, protein bars, gum, hard candy, socks, underwear, a hoodie, a flashlight, a lighter, a box of ammo for your pistol, a hunting knife, a toothbrush and travel toothpaste, and hand sanitizer. Not bad at all for a beginner."

Russ grinned at Brian. "Really, really good start. Let me give you a few more items. Follow me. Bring your bag." They went to the preps room, and the rest of us followed.

"Sorry about the mess," Russ said. "The boys are going to be working on straightening this up today."

I chimed in. "Janet and I will be helping them. We know where we want everything to go."

Russ laughed. "Admit it, Anne—your mild OCD won't let you *not* tell them where you want everything located." I stuck my tongue out at him. He blew me a kiss. Smart ass.

Russ went to the first shelf. He pulled out a mini water filter. He handed it to Brian. "This will filter any water source—up to a hundred thousand gallons, and 99.9999 percent of all bacteria. You can put the water in any bottle, stick the straw on the end of the filter, and drink it right from there." Brian looked it over, and added it to his bag. Russ moved over to the next shelf. He grabbed an emergency blanket and a breath mint tin.

"Um, if I have bad breath, you can just tell me," Brian said. "I brushed this morning, but I've had an electric toothbrush for years, so maybe I'm out of practice. Is bad breath an issue out there?"

We were all looking at him like he was slipping into minor insanity. Then, at almost the same time, we all burst out laughing.

Bob got control of himself first, and explained. "We make mini first aid kits out of those tins. After the mints are gone, we put in a few Band-Aids, some alcohol wipes, a bit of triple antibiotic cream, a needle and thread, some gauze and tape, a razor blade, and some waterproof matches. It isn't everything you would need in an emergency, but it could help. Russ, don't forget the 550 cord and duct tape."

Russ nodded and grabbed a small six-foot length of paracord and a lighter with duct tape wrapped around it. He handed all of that to Brian. Brian added them to his bag.

"Can you guys think of anything else? It's been a while since we put a BOB together." We all thought about it but didn't come up with anything more they needed. After all, they weren't going far—they shouldn't need anything but the water, and maybe a few energy bars.

With no more suggestions, Russ led us out to the garage. He wanted to make sure Rusty's bike was in good condition and the tires were aired up. After he verified the bike was ready to go, we went back in the house.

Russ looked at Bob. "We shouldn't be gone more than two hours. Does that sound about right, Brian?" Brian nodded. Russ continued. "If we aren't back in three, lock this place down, because anybody who could stop us would be too close to the house."

When he said that, I jerked my head up and looked at him, full of alarm. He put his arms around me to calm me down. "Babe, it's just a precaution. I'm sure we'll be fine. It shouldn't be bad out there yet. Some folks will probably have figured out what is going on and will be hunkered down at home. Some will still be waiting for someone to come help. A few will be causing problems, but those tend to be more active at night, since it's harder to see them coming. We probably won't run into anyone, but if we do, we'll see if they know anything. I promise, we'll be fine, and we'll be back soon. Keep the boys focused on the preps room. I love you, Anne."

With that, he kissed me, grabbed his bag, and headed back to the garage. Brian followed him. I watched as they looked out front and, apparently not seeing anyone, took the bikes around the fence and headed out to the woods behind the house. I took a breath that I was pretty sure I would be holding until they got back.

****

Since Brian had been through the woods on a pretty regular basis, Russ had him lead the way. He'd told him to take it slowly and keep his eyes and ears open for other people. Not being noticed was the game plan for longevity at the current location. Brian took it to heart, and was trying hard to stay alert for anything.

The path through the woods ran beside the main drag into town—well, the strip mall. "Into town" was a relative term. Fortunately, it was still within the tree line, so they could stay in the cover while they looked around. Brian noticed that all the cars

79

that he had seen the first day were still there. That made sense, as they were all pretty recent models. Different than the first day was the fact that many windows were broken, all the doors and trunks were open, and the cars looked like they had all been checked and ransacked. If there had been anything useful before, there wasn't now. There was no one around. He shared his previous experience with the area with Russ.

"There were a bunch of folks here when it happened, but nobody is here now. I hope everyone got home alright, especially those kids. That bus over there was about half full of teenagers. Who knows how many other kids—younger, like elementary school—might have been on buses when this happened. I'm glad I don't have kids. No offense, Russ."

Russ smiled at him. "None taken. We were fortunate that our kids hadn't gotten on the bus yet, or that first day would have gone down a lot different. And I'm with you—I hope those kids, and any others who weren't home, made it back. You can make yourself crazy thinking about what others are dealing with in these types of situations, but we can't worry about anyone but us now. It sucks, but you can't save everyone." Brian nodded in agreement. It did suck.

Russ had pulled out his binoculars and was scanning the area. He motioned to Brian. "Looks clear here. Let's try to get closer to the mall, but don't leave the woods. If we can do this without revealing ourselves to anyone, that's the preference."

The closer they got to the mall, the more evidence they saw on the streets of people—not people themselves, but signs that people had been there. Trash, lots of trash, the smell of decaying food, and—bodily fluids. Seriously? People were already peeing in the streets? Disgusting. Then they picked up the smell of smoke. Heavy smoke. That couldn't be good. They edged closer to the mall.

****

When they got close enough to see the mall, it was a shock. All the store windows were broken. While they couldn't see inside, they could tell from what was outside that the stores had been ransacked. There were broken bottles, empty food containers, broken appliances—none of the stores had been missed. Russ wasn't surprised. Those who hadn't been prepared for something like this would have panicked when they realized there were not going to be any more deliveries, at least not for the foreseeable future. There would have been a bunch of idiots who had stolen TVs and Blu-ray players. They wouldn't have figured out yet that those things were now worthless. They would have wasted their time stealing useless items when they should have been gathering food and water. But some people had figured that part out, because the grocery store was empty as well.

Scanning the mall with his binoculars, Russ spied a few people coming out of one of the stores. Probably looking for any scraps someone might have missed. *It could happen*, he thought. *There are things that could be eaten that some people might not have thought about—pet foods, for one. Yeah, sounds gross, unless you're really, really hungry. Dog food is made with meat, soy beans, grains—all things a human could ingest as well. Desperate times …*

As Russ looked around, he found the source of the strong smoke smell, a huge white cloud of it off to the right. He tracked it back to its source, and found what appeared to be an enormous fire. It looked like a whole neighborhood was burning. Actually, it probably was. If someone had tried to build a fire in their house to cook on, or to keep warm, and was careless, they could have set their house on fire. No fire department, no firetrucks, and the blaze would burn unimpeded. If the houses were close enough, and the wind was against them, it would spread to other houses. As if things weren't bad enough, the people from that area were now homeless as well. They also would have lost any supplies they had in the blaze. More desperation. This was not an area anyone would want to be around.

Russ told Brian what he'd seen and what his thoughts were on the area—that it was not a place they wanted to be seen around or near. "This place is five miles from our street, so it is easily a day's walk to the house. We need to get back, fast. Since the fire is still burning pretty fierce, the residents are probably still watching it, waiting for it to burn itself out, so they can check if there is anything left they can salvage. Once they find out there isn't, they'll start looking for empty houses close by. They'll work their way through those, then start on the ones that are occupied. They'll try asking at first, but after that, they'll take what they can. Anyone who can't protect and defend themselves is in trouble. Let's get back."

Brian took them back on a more direct path, at a quicker pace. Russ was trying to watch the ground for signs of traffic, to see if anyone had been through there. He didn't see anything, but that didn't mean no one had been there. Tracking wasn't his best skill. He just wanted to get home as fast as he could, because he needed to be where he could protect his family.

When they got to the edge of the woods closest to the house, they stopped and scanned the area. They didn't see anything out of place, or anybody else, so they went on to the house. They were met in the garage by the family, all very relieved they were back. Russ hugged everyone, then turned to the group.

"Gang, we may not have as long as I was hoping we would. There are a bunch of houses up by the mall that are burning down. The people who lived there will be looking for housing, but more importantly, food. It won't take them long to work their way through the houses between there and here. We may have a week, two at the most. We have to get the trailers loaded. We're bugging out in a week, no more."

# Chapter 7

Russ filled us in on their trip over lunch. We were still eating pretty rich, since things were still thawing, so we had cooked steaks out on the grill. Russ told us he had smelled the food cooking while they were still about a half-mile away. Right then, no more cooking outside. Russ and Brian's field trip had served another purpose. Hopefully, the smoke from the burning neighborhood up the road would disguise the cooking smells if anyone was close—which we were really hoping wasn't the case.

"All the stores at the mall have been cleaned out. The road is covered with cars that aren't going anywhere. That will slow us down getting to the farm. We may have to move vehicles out of the way. That will also be dangerous—any time we have to stop, once we get on the road, we will be susceptible to attack. People see two vehicles, pulling trailers, that run? They are going to want it all. We have to have a plan before we hit the road. For now, we need to start packing everything up in here to get it loaded. Ladies, I suggest you start packing clothes for everyone. Us guys and the boys will work on the supplies for the trailers."

While we were glad that we would eventually be at the farm, which was our final destination, we weren't happy about the changes to our plan. We hadn't wanted to be rushed when we left. There was always a chance of forgetting something when you were in a hurry. For this reason, I had made lists, with Russ's input, and they would hopefully cover everything we needed to do.

I went to the desk and grabbed the folder titled "SHTF." Inside, I had a list of supplies and where they were in the house. Some of the things were not necessarily in the preps room. I had a list of tasks that we needed to complete before we left. I had a list of things we might find useful on the trip to the farm. The last list was of who would do what. A little OCD, but in a good way.

"Okay, gang, here's everything we need to do or gather for our trip to the farm. I think if we split it up, we can do it all in two days. Will that be fast enough, baby?" I looked to Russ for confirmation.

He smiled and nodded. "Let's get busy then."

\*\*\*\*

We spent the rest of the day working our butts off to get things done. We made a really big dent in the lists, working at a rate that would see us done the next afternoon. Just after dark, we collapsed all over the living room, in chairs, on the floor—we weren't picky.

We were dirty and sweaty, and we all needed a shower. Janet and I decided we'd go first, then we could throw something together for supper while the guys got cleaned up. Janet told me to go first, and I didn't argue.

I went upstairs, grabbed some clothes, and headed to the bathroom. I turned the water on, shucked my nasty clothes, and stepped into the shower. As soon as I got done lathering up, the water stopped. No. Freaking. Way. *Now? The water stops now?* I grabbed a towel, wrapped it around my soapy self, leaned out the door, and yelled, "Russ! Help!" Russ was at the door in like five seconds.

"Anne! What is it? What's wrong?" He looked at me and grimaced. "No water?"

I gave him a snarky reply. "How'd you know? Did the lather give it away?" He laughed. "Hang tight. I'll be right back."

Russ was back in just a few minutes with one of the sun showers. We'd been leaving them out in the sun, since we didn't know how long the water would last. "There's only about four gallons of water in here, so just leave it on long enough to rinse off. We have four sun showers, and seven people who need a shower. I'll go down and tell everyone we need to modify our shower methods."

With the little shower hanging from the main shower head, it had decent gravitational pressure. I switched the valve open and got a bit of water on myself to dampen the now-dry soap. I quickly closed the valve, re-lathered, scraped off as much of the soap suds as I could by hand, and turned the valve open again. I hoped I had left at least a gallon of water, maybe a little more for Janet. She'd need another sun shower bag to finish off, but if we did it right, we could get through seven people with the four we had. Maybe.

I got dressed, got a comb through my hair—since I hadn't had a chance to condition it was kind of tangled—and went downstairs. Everyone was waiting for my verdict on the sun shower.

"If you get wet quick, shut off the water, lather up, scrape off the suds, and rinse quick, we can probably get all of us a shower. Janet, you're next—but she'll need another bag, Russ."

Russ was heading for the back door. Brian stopped him. "Russ, I have two fifty-gallon gas water heaters at my house. The gas is still on, which means I have a hundred gallons of hot water over there. Is there any way we can use that?" Russ and Bob looked at each other, and seemed to get the same idea at the same time. They were freaky like that sometimes.

Bob chimed in. "I think we can, Brian. We're going to need a lot of hose, so we can reach from your house to the fence. Us guys can do an outdoor shower, like the military. It's dark, no one will see us—not that we really care." He laughed at the idea, and the other fellas joined in. Men were so uninhibited. It probably came from being able to pee anywhere.

Russ brought in the next sun shower and gave it to Bob. He went upstairs with Janet and got her fixed up. While he was doing that, Russ and Brian worked on the "guy" shower set up. As I was thinking about dinner, I got an idea. I went out back and called to Russ. He came running.

"Is something wrong, babe?"

"No, no, nothing's wrong. I just had an idea. Can you rig up a faucet on that hose, so we can use the water from Brian's for other things? We really need to wash clothes before we head out if we can. Hot water would help with that."

He thought for a minute. "I think we can. I'll talk to Bob, and we'll get it set up." He headed back out to the guys.

I whipped up some soup and grilled cheese sandwiches on the camp stove set up in the kitchen. Not the safest with the gas canisters, but safer than someone outside smelling our food cooking. By the time everyone got done with their showers, they would all be ready for food. I think the guys must have had a good time with what they rigged up, because they all came in laughing and dripping.

I took one look at them and shook my head. "Did you guys use the entire hundred gallons? I would have thought it would be too hot for you to use directly." I went to the laundry room, grabbed a bunch of towels, and passed them out.

Brian smiled at me, and grinned at the guys. "Apparently the gas has shut down too. The water was almost the perfect temp. We might have used a little more than we meant to, but there should still be a full fifty gallons for laundry duty. If it helps, we kind of washed our smelly clothes we were wearing while we showered."

They all started laughing again. I looked at them like they were all drunk—and they might have been, at least the grown-ups. I was sure I smelled booze.

"And what else did you guys get from over there? What did you do with your clothes?" They pointed out the door; I leaned out and looked. The clothes line was covered. Not really hung properly, more like tossed onto the lines. Oh well, at least they were semi clean.

"Fine. Since you did laundry, you're forgiven for drinking without me and Janet. Besides, you're going to sober up when you eat. Coffee to follow. Strong coffee."

They were grinning like they had won the lottery or something. I shook my head and pointed to the table. They sat down and started eating. Right then Janet came down, looking quite refreshed. She saw that I had taken care of dinner and frowned at me.

"Anne, you shouldn't have done all that by yourself. I'm sorry I took so long. When the guys said they had an alternative, I went ahead and used all the water in the sun shower bags. It was much better than I thought it would be. What can I do now?"

I smiled at my friend and threw an arm over her shoulder. "You can sit down with the rest of us and eat. You've done most of the cooking the past couple of days, so you were due for a pass. Let's eat, before the guys devour it all."

We had a nice dinner, followed by the promised coffee. By the time we had finished, the men were sober, and the boys were falling asleep. We sent them up to bed. They had worked their butts off and needed to get a good night's sleep. Tomorrow would probably be just as busy. Brian, Russ, and Bob decided to keep their security schedule the same, so Brian was up first. As his was probably the easiest one to serve, we felt he could handle it alone. Janet and I put our foot down with Bob and Russ though. We told them we were going to be up with them. We would keep them in coffee and give them another set of eyes, probably out back. They didn't like it but did see the logic behind it.

With Brian set up with a thermos of coffee, the rest of us went upstairs to try to get some sleep. That probably wouldn't be too hard, since we had had a very physical day. It would be harder to wake up. But we had to—wake up, that is. We couldn't afford to lose our supplies, and that threat was coming closer.

****

Brian heard them before he saw them. Not really stealthy there, guys. Same pickup truck, from the sound of it. It was just before 1:00 a.m., and dark as a black hole outside. Since it was almost time for Bob's shift, he crept up the stairs and knocked on his and Janet's door. Bob came to the door almost instantly.

"Hey, buddy, give me a sec to throw a shirt on, and I'll be right down."

Brian looked at him and gave him a curt nod. "Grab your boots, too. I think we've got company coming."

Bob jerked his head up with a start. "Where? How many?"

Brian shook his head. "I'm not sure. I haven't seen them yet. I just heard something out front. Should we get Russ up?"

Bob responded softly. "Let's see what we're dealing with before we wake the house up." With that decided, they headed down to the living room.

Still black as coal outside, with the new moon phase, it was a perfect time for someone to be out scavenging, since no one would be able to see them. Of course, that worked both ways—they wouldn't be able to see anyone else either.

Brian peered through the window shutters, Bob next to him, and saw a flash of light. Actually, it was a flashlight. There was someone in the yard of the house across the street. They seemed to be going from window to window, looking inside. Definitely not the Nelsons, who lived there. There hadn't been any sign of them since everything went down. They both worked the 7:00 a.m. to 3:00 p.m. shift at a plastic container plant on the other side of town. It was a good thirty miles away; with a car that was only about three years old, the only way they were getting home was walking. They probably could have done that in the time that had passed, so things weren't looking good for them. They were young and lived in the today. They ate out four or five nights a week, so there probably weren't a whole lot of supplies in the house. If you're hungry, though, anything is better than starving.

Brian tried to count how many were out there. It looked like four, but there could have been some on the back side of the house, or even other groups their size, checking other houses. They needed to get everybody up, but as quietly as possible—and without lights. No sense bringing attention to themselves if someone out there was looking our way.

**\*\*\*\***

There was a knock on our bedroom door, waking us instantly. "Russ, we got company outside." It was Brian; Russ was at the door, dressed from head to toe, with his S&W .40 pistol and his Mossberg 500 shotgun, in just a matter of seconds. The group was sleeping in comfortable clothes these days, but clothes you could walk out the door and leave in if you had to. He opened the door and looked at Brian.

"Where? How many?"

Brian gave him a slight smile. "That's exactly what Bob asked. You guys are brothers from another mother, aren't you?"

Brian looked grim as he relayed what he and Bob had seen. Russ turned to me. "Grab your nine-millimeter and the .308 rifle.

No lights, no candles, no lamps. Tell the boys to keep it quiet, but get everybody downstairs, armed." I nodded, finished putting my hiking boots on, grabbed the guns, and headed for the boys' room.

Janet and Bob were there already, getting the boys up, dressed, and packing, and I don't mean a suitcase. They both had nine-millimeter pistols and were quite proficient with them. Rusty had a Beretta 92FS; Ben's was a Taurus 111G2. Mine was a Beretta Px4 Storm subcompact. Bob carried a Glock 22, chambered in .40, like Russ's S&W. Janet carried a Glock 17, which was a nine-millimeter, like mine and the boys'. We were able to keep the majority of our ammo in two calibers for the pistols this way. We all had belts that held at least three extra magazines. At fifteen or more rounds per mag, that gave us at least sixty shots if we needed them. I hoped and prayed we wouldn't.

We headed down the stairs to the living room. As we rounded the corner, Russ was holding up a hand, telling us to stay put. Bob ducked down and kind of squat-walked over to where Russ and Brian were standing. I motioned the boys behind me, as well as Janet. I leaned out and peeked around the corner at the guys. Russ was looking out the shutter crack with his night vision monocular. As dark as it was, this was the perfect time to use it. He must have pulled it out of the Faraday cage while we were getting everyone ready upstairs. It wasn't military grade, but it worked, and right then it was a life saver. He looked at Brian and Bob and held up four fingers. Four people out there. Doing what? I wanted to go to the window so badly, to see for myself, but when it came to threat assessment, Russ was in charge. He left Bob and Brian at the window and came back to where we were waiting.

"I see four people casing the Nelson house. It doesn't look like they have broken in yet, but we don't know that for sure. We also don't know if there are any more with them, maybe in the back of the house, or even at a different house we can't see from here. For now, we're going to watch these guys, but we are also going to look for any others. I'll take the front, Bob is going to take the back, Brian will watch the side closest to his house so he can keep an eye on his place as well. I want you guys to first go around to all the windows and make sure the blinds are closed, front side up. Then draw the curtains tight. After that, head upstairs and do the same with the windows up there. I'm hoping if they can't see in they won't break in—for now. At some point, they will start breaking into all of them, looking for food and water, possibly a place to squat for a while if there is a good amount of supplies. They'll hit the ones they know are empty first. Then they'll move on to the ones someone else is in. That's when it will get ugly. That's why we want to be gone before it gets to that point. Each of you take a side of the house from up there, but be careful not to open the blinds. Just slide one slat up at the edge to look out through. It's pitch black out there, but they seem to all have a light source of some kind, so you can find them that way. You'll be able to see further from up there, so look out past the next house or the fence. Keep track of how many you see. If nothing happens and they just move on, we'll meet up in about an hour to compare notes. If they break into the Nelson place, or any other you can see from up there, come down and let us know. Any questions?"

Everyone shook their heads. "Alright, then head upstairs as soon as you check the windows down here. If you see anything outside of them just looking into houses, come get us."

We each headed to a separate room downstairs. We had installed plantation blinds on all the windows in the house, along with pretty dark curtains. With the blinds closed up, no one could see in the house. Since everything had shut down, we had made a habit of checking them at night before we went to bed, as we were apt to open them a bit for the natural light source during the day, at least on the back side of the house. Even though I was sure we had checked before going to bed a few hours ago, we checked again. Better safe than really sorry. After we verified the blinds were closed downstairs, we headed up. From the second story we could see for a pretty good distance across the whole area. It was a good spot to use to check the neighborhood.

When we got upstairs, Janet took the front of the house. That would give her a view of the Nelson house, as well as the houses on either side of theirs. I took the view over the garage, which also let me see Bob and Janet's place and the street coming into the neighborhood. Rusty took the opposite side, which covered Brian's house and the end of the street. It ended just past his house. Ben took the back of the house, which didn't include other homes, but did have a good view of the woods past the backyard fence. Between the four or us, we had a pretty full 360-degree view of the surrounding area. If anyone else was out there, we should be able to see them, if they were using a light source.

While we were getting situated upstairs, the guys were positioning themselves on the first floor. We didn't have a view to Bob and Janet's down there, because of the garage, so they only had three directions to monitor. Russ had the front, Bob the back. Brian had an unobstructed view of the side to his house. He didn't have binoculars, but with no light noise, his eyes adjusted pretty quickly to the dark. He peered through the slat in the blinds, trying to see something, anything, in that direction. There was no movement that he could detect. Not that he had left anything over there for anyone to loot, but if things didn't stay like they were now, he'd like to have a home he could move back into without a lot of work—you know, broken windows, kicked-in doors, that kind of thing.

Bob had the back, which wasn't a lot to see, since he was looking at the backyard, which was enclosed in a privacy fence. He wasn't seeing past that fence. He could, however, see anyone who climbed over the fence into the backyard. Lord help them if they did. He went out into the sunroom to give a listen. With no electrical sounds, or vehicles, any other noise would carry well. He stayed out there for a bit. As dark as it was, no one was going to see him anyway, unless they shined a light on him.

Russ had the most action, out front. There were no more people, and the ones at the Nelsons' didn't actually break in. They finished their recon and then moved to the house next door. Were they working one side of the street, then moving to the other side, our side? Just in case, we had plantation blinds behind the shutters, so there was no chance they were seeing inside. We had tested it ourselves. Russ would see them coming—or Brian, depending on which side they came to first. They'd have to climb the fence to see in the back, and Bob would see them before they saw him. He only had to slip inside the door, and he was shielded from outside view.

Upstairs, we didn't see any other people besides the four at the Nelson house. That was good news—this wasn't a big crew. We hoped it stayed that way. There was strength in numbers. That's why we'd brought Brian into the fold. The bad guys, the desperate, they'd all figure that out as well. As time went by, there would be fewer single-family units and more multi-family groups. The thing is, family isn't necessarily blood. We were all family in that house—us, the Hoppers, now Brian. When other "families" got together, they wouldn't always be for the good of others. Things like that were why we were planning to leave and head to the farm when we felt it was relatively safe. Although there would come a point where nothing, nowhere, was safe.

After about an hour, we met up downstairs. We all reported no more sightings, other than the four at the Nelson house. Since

Russ had had the best view from downstairs, he relayed his findings first.

"I only saw the four. They didn't break in, that I saw, but I'll bet they'll be back. The Nelsons didn't keep their blinds drawn, so those folks should have been able to see in pretty easy. Whether or not they have anything worth taking, we don't know. But soon it won't matter. All those houses that burned up by the mall had people living in them. Any of those people who happened to be home when this went down, or were able to get home, are looking for food, water, and shelter. That place represents two, possibly three of those needs, depending on how big their hot-water heater is, and if they had any bottled water over there. Once those resources are used up, they'll move on to the next house. That could be ours. No, I'm not ready for us to bug out yet, but if we don't go soon, we may be put in a position that we have to defend this place. These guys could be a part of a larger group. They could have been scouting the area for a migration. If that happens, we absolutely want to be gone. Did any of you see anything from upstairs, anyone else?" We all shook our heads. No activity at any of the houses we could see.

"Okay, then we need to try to get some sleep, at least a couple of hours. Bob is on watch, but I'm going to stay up with him, just to have another set of eyes on the side of the house that leads out to the road. Janet, if you'll bunk in with Anne, we can put the boys in your room, and I can use their room to keep an eye out from upstairs. Is that cool?" Janet nodded. I really didn't think we'd be getting a lot of sleep, but at least we could have some girl time, talk about what had happened. The boys could sleep through anything.

"Can we at least make you guys a fresh pot of coffee?" I try to take care of my man, my men.

They both grinned at me. Bob responded first. "Yes, dear, you most certainly can." We laughed, a much needed laugh, and Janet and I headed for the kitchen. It had been a long night already, and it wasn't over. Unfortunately, it looked like this might be the first of a whole lot of long nights to come. What we didn't know, or expect, was that the latest challenge would come from a source closer to home. Because of that, it would be a lot more personal, for all of us.

# Chapter 8

The Baxters lived on the other side of Bob and Janet. We were not friends with them. Dan and Lucy had bought the house in a foreclosure sale. When they first moved in, Dan had been running a landscaping business from home, while Lucy was an elementary school teacher. They had a grown daughter who lived with them, Lacy, who had a twelve-year-old daughter herself, Laney. Their grown son, Don, lived with them as well. It wasn't too long before Dan stopped landscaping and Lucy stopped teaching. Neither of their kids had jobs. It was a mystery in the neighborhood how they lived with four grown-ups in the house, none of whom worked. We had our suspicions that Don was dealing drugs, as there were cars coming and going all hours of the evening and night. Between that and the state aid Lacy would be getting for Laney, it was possible they could have held on to the house.

They were what we called "white trash." The grown-up kids would scream at each other inside the house, yet you could hear it two doors down at our place if you were out in the yard. They never came out of the house until late afternoon or early evening, except to take Laney to school. They seemed to go to the grocery store every evening. This was the part we felt would be a problem in the situation we now found ourselves in. If they had to go to the store every day, they would have little to no food stores in the house. When what little they had was gone, they would be looking for "help."

When we had sat down together with Bob and Janet and tried to think about what all could happen here at home, the Baxters always came up. Russ and Bob were adamant that we would not be helping them in any way. Janet and I were concerned for the child, but the guys were firm.

"Anne, we have our own kids to take care of. She isn't our responsibility. If something happens and it lasts for months, or even years, we can't take them on to raise. Our families come first. I'm sorry if that's harsh, or that makes me an asshole, but there will be a lot of people out there like the Baxters who never did anything in the way of planning for a disaster. We can't take care of all of them, so we won't take care of any of them."

I could hear that discussion like it was yesterday. At the time, I think I believed nothing would really happen. Now that it had, I knew what he meant. If my giving them food because they had a child meant Rusty went without, it was a no-brainer.

We hadn't cooked anything outside since the day before, when Russ let us know how far away the smell had been picked up. However, this was day three, so the Baxters were probably out of food. None of us had brought them up, but when the knock came at the front door, and the guys went to see who it was, I can't say I was surprised to find out it was Dan. He had Don with him.

Russ opened the door, with his pistol openly in its holster. Bob and Brian joined him, equally openly armed. They all walked out on the porch and closed the door behind them. I knew why. None of them wanted the Baxters to see inside our house, to see what we had. Janet and I decided to make sure we kept the view from the front door in mind going forward, when we had supplies out. For that matter, we'd mind the view from the back door, too. We went to the window to watch the show.

Russ took the offensive. "Can we help you fellas?" Dan looked at Russ with a bit of a cocky tilt to his head. "Yes, you can. We got no idea what's going on, but we haven't had any power for three days. I got no notion how long this is going to last. We can't even get a car to turn on so we can check the radio for info. Do you guys know what this is all about?"

Russ shook his head. "We are in the same boat you are. We don't know anything and haven't been able to get anything on a radio either." Not really a lie, since we had a radio that worked, but we hadn't heard a damn thing on it. Bob and Brian nodded in agreement.

Dan continued. "Well, since we don't have a car that runs, we can't get to the store to get any food, and we're pretty much out. Can you all help us out? Just give us something to tide us over a few days until everything gets fixed?" Yep, clueless, just like we had thought. In their defense though, I would bet less than 25 percent of the population had any idea what was really happening. Everyone was so used to electricity, cable TV, Wi-Fi, and running water, they couldn't fathom life without it. At least not for very long.

Russ shook his head a second time. "Again, we're in the same boat you are. Everybody is. We don't have anything we can spare. I'm sorry."

Don decided to jump in. "We smelled your grill cooking the other day. You have food. You should do the decent thing and share it with your neighbors."

Bob jumped in himself. "Have you smelled it since then? We cooked what was in the freezer thawing out so it wouldn't ruin. We're doing ramen noodles now, and those are about gone."

Dan was eyeing the guys' sidearms. "Why are you guys carrying guns? What do you think this is, the Wild West?" He and Don shared a laugh.

"Not yet," Brian said. "But what do you think is going to happen in a few more days if nothing comes back on? How many more people do you think are out there like you, trying to get someone to help them? What do you think they'll do when they don't get any help? They'll try to take what other people have. You'll have to fight to keep what you have, to survive."

Don sneered at Brian. "What do you have that you need to protect? This isn't even your house. Don't you live over there?" He jerked his head in the direction of Brian's house.

Russ took over. "Brian is staying with us, so we can watch each other's backs. Things will very likely get ugly in the not-too-distant future, and we are going to deal with it together."

Dan spoke up again. "Well, we can help you fellas with that. We can watch out for each other. You help us, we'll help you. Like him."

Bob stepped forward, getting into Dan's personal space. "We don't need your help. We're covered. You boys need to get on home and try to figure something out for your family to eat. Maybe you could set some snares in the woods back there and try to get a rabbit or squirrel. We can't help you."

Dan took a slight step back but didn't give up his ground. He stared into Bob's eyes. "So, that's how it is then? We know you got food in there—none of you look hungry. You just gonna stand by while my granddaughter starves to death? She's just a little girl. She didn't ask for this! You could at least give us something for her."

There it was, the last card they had to play: the guilt card.

Russ had heard enough. "Do you think for one second I care more about your granddaughter being hungry than *my son*? You and your people mean *nothing* to me! You are *not* my responsibility. It is not my fault that you planned no further ahead than the next day when you went to the grocery store. I'd suggest you go figure out some way to feed your family that does not include taking from mine. I think it's time for you to leave. *Now*."

With the anger in Russ's voice and the threatening stance he had taken, Bob and Brian closed ranks with him. Dan and Don backpedaled off the porch and into the yard.

Don had a look of pure hatred on his face as he sputtered, "You can't just let us starve! You have to help! What about those chickens and rabbits you got out back? You could give us a couple of those!"

Bob walked down and stuck his face in Don's. "Like Russ said, we got our own kids to feed. You are *not* our problem. And if any of those animals come up missing, your door is the first one we'll be at. You understand me, boy?"

Dan put his hand on his son's arm and pulled him back. "We understand. We're going. To hell with all of you."

They turned and headed back down the street toward their house. Every few steps, Don looked back over his shoulder at our house. Right before he went in the door, he turned back and flipped the guys off. Real mature.

The guys watched them all the way, until they were back in their own house. Bob looked at Russ. "You know this isn't over, right? They just aren't hungry enough yet."

Russ nodded. "Yep, you're right. They'll be back, and they won't be knocking on the door. Let's move the animals into the garage. This just keeps getting better."

# Chapter 9

Morning brought no new news. The scavengers had left without entering the Nelson house, so we felt like we might have a slight breather. Not that they may not come back—in fact they probably would, as early as that night—but for now it was quiet on our street again. Brian wanted to make sure his place was not easily viewed from outside, after seeing the people casing the Nelsons', so he, Russ, and Bob decided to check his house, the Nelson place, and the next house up from them. They grabbed their sidearms and shotguns and a cup of coffee and headed out. The boys and us gals continued working on loading the trailers.

The trailers were big, seven by sixteen, and almost six feet inside height. That was almost six hundred cubic feet of space. The floors had been reinforced and the axles swapped out for the heaviest load capacity the guys could find. We could load them front to back, floor to ceiling with supplies and not have to worry about the weight. The challenge was getting the most use of the space. That's where Janet and I came in.

I'm one of those people who rearrange the dishwasher when someone else loads it. You can call me OCD if you want, but it's more about getting the most dishes in and still having them all come out clean. It was a puzzle, and I love puzzles. Tetris was one of my favorite video games. Janet was a kindred spirit as a puzzle lover, so she took one trailer and I took the other, with our respective kids doing the heavy lifting.

We started with the bulk basics—flour, sugar, rice, beans—and had them stacked and packed in the front of the trailers. We knew we needed the weight on the tongue. We had some room at the tops, so we stuffed blankets, sheets, pillows, and towels up there. Who cares what that stuff looks like when you pull it out? Next were cases of canned goods—soups, veggies, pastas—with bags of clothes on top of them. We left room in the back of the trailers for tools and anything else the guys needed to bring. They had about 25 percent of the floor space to fill with their "stuff." We could get them a bit more if needed, but we basically had all the food, clothes, linens, cooking implements, utensils, first aid kits, and anything else we could do without for now, loaded in the trailers. There were tents, sleeping bags, and cots, but no mattresses or beds. We had those things already set up at the farm, so what we were bringing with us was for emergencies or group growth. We had an idea of who would be with us there, but that could change, as in the case of Brian. We left ourselves open to increasing our numbers. There was strength in numbers.

We loaded up most of the propane canisters for the camp stoves, leaving a few for use there at the houses. We put two of the four stoves in the trailers and kept two out for cooking. We kept enough food for at least a month in the house. We probably wouldn't need that much—it wasn't looking like we were going to be there that long after all. We did still have space in the back of the trucks, so we could throw whatever we had left in there when we bugged out. We had enough water in the waterBOBs to cover our needs for cooking and cleaning, so we packed up the rest of the bottled water, along with all but two of the filters. Janet and I looked around for anything we might have missed. Outside of what we were using daily, or multiple times a day, we had everything else loaded. We could bug out in less than an hour. With the big work done, we put a pot of coffee on to brew. We deserved a break.

****

While we were plotting the loading of the trailers, the guys were scoping out Brian's place. Russ said he had done a surprisingly good job of shutting it up pretty tight; they only found a couple of windows that revealed a view into the house. Brian unlocked the door, and they went in and let the blinds down all the way on all the windows. They did a quick sweep of the house, just to make sure no one had gotten in without being noticed. Everything looked just like he'd left it.

"Hey, guys, I thought about something I left here. Give me a minute." Brian headed for the stairs.

Bob hollered his way. "If it's more wine, we'll help you carry it." They laughed and followed him.

He went into his spare room, which he had set up as a remote office. He opened the closet door and pulled out a small container, like a paint can. It was heavy, and he needed both hands to pick it up. Russ and Bob looked at it with raised eyebrows.

"I've been saving change for like ten years," Brian said. "I have four of these. I figure even if paper money is worthless, the silver should have some value, right?" He looked to the guys for confirmation. They were both nodding.

"Anything before 1964? Those are almost pure silver. Even the later stuff will have some value. What made you think of that?" Russ was eying him; Brian thought he looked impressed.

Brian smiled at them. "There's probably some older stuff in there, but I never really looked at any of it. I just threw it in the can. As for what made me think of it, there's this three-hour time span at night I'm up by myself, looking out at the dark. Most of the time, there's nothing to see. So, I got one of Anne's e-readers out of the Faraday cage, and I've been reading up on stuff. Prepping, survival, homesteading—she's got tons of books. I had no idea there was so much to learn about living without the conveniences of a modern world. I am so lucky to have been living next door to you guys when this happened. That you agreed to include me in your plans is like the best thing that could have happened to me. I want to do whatever I can to help us get where we're going, as easy as possible. I don't have nearly the supplies you guys have, so I am looking for any way I can find to help out. This change might be an asset at some point. Let's get it over to the house." Brian already thought of the house as his, and of the rest of the guys as his family.

The guys grabbed the cans and hauled them down the stairs. Brian did a quick run through the kitchen for any other food stuffs he might have missed. There weren't any. If anyone broke in here, they were going to be out of luck. They might have a roof, but no food or water. Hell, not even any wine—they grabbed the last six bottles, wrapped them in kitchen towels, and took them as well. There was a clothes basket in the laundry room, and they used that to carry the wine and one of the coin buckets. With each one carrying a bucket, and Russ and Bob sharing the handling of the basket, they left the house.

Brian locked the door behind him, knowing there was a good chance he'd never be back. It didn't matter. That life was gone. A new one was starting, about which he had a lot to learn, but he was excited at the prospect. And scared, to an extent. He had no idea what the future held, for any of them. No one did. They were definitely on a new, untraveled path here. At least he wasn't on it alone.

As they were coming up on the porch back at the house, they heard a familiar sound. The old truck from the other day. Shit. Those guys were back. The question was, were they the same ones who had come the night before? Was there one potential threat, or two?

# Chapter 10

I heard the guys coming in the front door at almost the same time I heard the truck. They quickly got in and shut the door, set down the stuff they had brought over—did I see more wine? Score!—and went to the shutters on the front windows. Since the events of the night before, or rather early that morning, we hadn't opened any of the blinds.

The truck slowed down in front of the house, then turned into the Nelsons' driveway. So, either they were a part of the group from the night before, they *were* the ones from the night before, or everybody in the area had their eye on the Nelson house. I can't say option three was high on my list—everyone knew they ate out most nights, so there was no way there were a lot of supplies over there. That left the guys we saw the night before, or part of a group they were all in. Either way, if they were coming back in daylight, they had seen something they wanted in there. Bad.

I went to Russ. "Did you guys get a chance to go over there and see what you could see through the windows?"

He shook his head. "No, we grabbed some things at Brian's after we checked the windows, and as we were bringing the stuff here, we heard the truck coming down the street. We barely got in when it rounded the corner. What the hell could they have over there that would make them come back during the day to get it? Those two are millennials, they live in the moment. No way there is anything of use over there, is there?"

I couldn't imagine what could be over there, but then again we hadn't really known them well. Once we'd started down the prepper path, we had a tendency to keep a buffer zone between us and the rest of the neighborhood, besides Bob and Janet. You didn't want just anybody knowing you were a prepper, or that you had a lot of supplies. A smile, a wave, a hello if you saw them outside, but no barbeques, or pot lucks, or neighborhood watch groups—in an apocalyptic event, neighbors become predators. The less they knew about us, the safer our family was. The flip side to that was we didn't know any more about them than they knew about us.

We gathered at the shutters and watched the truck. After a minute, the driver's door opened, and a man who appeared to be in his mid-thirties got out. He looked around, up and down the street, then spoke to the guy in the passenger seat. He got out on his side, sporting a shotgun, and looked over the area as well. Another man got out of the truck, and all three headed toward the backyard. Well, at least they had the decency to break in from the back, instead of brazenly kicking in the front door. Those actions would come later, when things got more desperate. For now, they would try to hide their illegal entry to some extent.

It was only a few minutes until the guy from the middle seat came back to the truck, carrying a duffel bag. While we couldn't see what all was in it, we saw the barrels of a few guns sticking out the end. So that was it. Aaron Nelson had guns. Probably had a gun rack in the living room, with the rifles or shotguns on display. Yeah, that would have been worth risking a daylight robbery.

The guy from the passenger side came out with a box that looked pretty heavy. Though we couldn't see inside it, the guess was either canned goods or ammo—or both. The driver came out last, carrying what looked like a large range bag. From the way he was carrying it, it appeared to be pretty heavy as well. Handguns and ammo were a safe bet. They put their loot into the back of the truck, loaded up, and backed out into the street. They stopped and looked toward our house. We instinctively all took a step back. No way they could see us, especially during the day, but it was a reflex. They sat idling for a minute, looking our way and talking to each other. We had no way of knowing what they were saying, but it couldn't have been good. It could mean our place was next on their list.

They put the truck in gear and headed back out of the neighborhood. Russ turned to us with a grim look.

"They'll be back, and they'll be coming here. We need to get everything locked up tight, inside and out. We can't chance leaving without knowing where they are staying. They obviously aren't walking distance close. So, we're going to try to ride this out for now. But we need to get a few things done. As soon as we know they're gone, we'll get busy." I had no idea what else we needed to do. Russ did, and he'd help us get it done.

****

We waited an hour but didn't see any sign of any more "visitors" to the neighborhood. Russ and Bob had been out back, checking on the trailers. They were proud of the work we'd done getting them loaded. Now we needed to make sure no one got them. When they were pretty sure we were alone, they pulled Russ's truck out of the garage and took it out back. The plan was to move them against the back fence, with the doors against the fence, padlocked. Then they put hitch locks on them, so no one could hook up to them and take them. Lastly, they took some stuff from around the yard and leaned it up against the trailers, so it looked like they had been there a while, at least at a casual glance. Maybe it would be enough. They pulled the distributor cap off Bob's truck, removed the rotor button, and replaced the cap, after they pulled it in sideways in front of the trailers. Pretty good chance no one was carrying a spare with them. That would make his truck theft-proof, better than The Club any day.

When they came back in, Brian spoke up. "Guys, I think we should go over and take a look at what they did at the Nelsons'. We might be able to figure out what they took, to some extent. We should at least check it out."

Russ and Bob agreed, but Bob added a thought. "Just in case they come back, we shouldn't move anything. We don't want them to know there's anyone else around."

They grabbed their sidearms, and Russ went out to the garage to get the two two-way radios stored in the Faraday cabinet. He came back in and handed one to me. "Keep an eye out front. Janet, you go upstairs and watch from the boys' room. You can open the blinds a bit during the day. If you see anything, or anybody that isn't us, call me on the radio. We'll be back in a few." He gave me a kiss, and they went out the front.

***

In the yard, they stopped to look and listen. They didn't see or hear anything besides birds and squirrels, so they headed across the street. As they got closer to the house, they were looking for any signs of breaking and entering. They were pretty sure it had all been done in the back, but they wanted a full picture of what had happened. Brian went up to the window that would look into the living room. The blinds were opened enough that he had a good view of the fireplace area. Next to the fireplace was a gun case, empty. The glass had been shattered, and it looked like there were at least a half dozen rifles or shotguns missing. He called Russ and Bob over to see the mess. They all took a look, then headed around back.

The damage was immediately evident. The back door had been kicked in, with no care for the damage done. They walked through the doorway, stepping on broken glass and splintered wood. The door went into the kitchen, where all the cabinet doors were open to empty shelves. It looked like the men had flung everything out into the floor, with no care to what was destroyed. There were busted dishes all over the counter. There was a small pantry on the other wall that was standing open. It had definitely been ransacked, but surprisingly there were a few things left that would be very valuable in the coming days—flour, sugar, coffee, tea. Dumbasses. They probably grabbed all the microwave mac and cheese, not even getting that they had no microwave to cook it in. If they didn't see the value in flour and sugar, they would probably never figure out how to cook without a microwave.

Brian started to grab what was left, but Russ stopped him. "Leave it. We have plenty, and someone may come through who can use it." Brian nodded, and moved on to the next cabinet.

They went down the hall, looking into each room as they passed them. At the master bedroom, the closet door was open. It looked like they had found ammo in there, as there were some empty cartridge boxes on the floor. The jewelry box on the dresser

117

was flipped on its side, empty. If Laura had any jewelry worth something that wasn't on her, they'd got that. The fellas went back toward the living room and stopped at the door of one of the bedrooms. There was a large gun cabinet in there. It was locked, a combination lock. There was a good chance it was full of guns, and an even better chance the looters would be back to try to get into it. Great.

The guys headed out the back door, trying to keep from leaving any trace of their having been there. They stopped outside, and Russ pulled out his radio.

"How's it looking out there, babe?"

I called up to Janet, who hadn't seen anything; nor had I. I radioed back to Russ, "All clear that we can see. Come on home."

Russ came back, "On our way." They rushed across the road to the house.

They got inside and closed and locked the door. They told us what they had seen over there. We spent the rest of the day talking about what had happened, but more about what could happen. What would people like that do if they broke in here, with us still at home? What would they do to us, or us to them? It would not be a win for anyone. Everyone's safety was at risk. It scared the hell out of all of us. We were going to have to decide when we were going, soon.

****

Dinner was soup and sandwiches again. We still needed to use up the bread, and soup could feed a lot of folks with a few ingredients. The things in the freezer were no longer frozen, but still cold. We had cooked most of the chicken in soups. Pork and beef would last a few more days uncooked than the chicken would, so we were trying to finish it up. This would be the last batch of chicken soup until we got to the farm. We had more chicken that was canned and dehydrated, but we needed to use up the fresh stuff first. I thought the next big batch of something we made would probably be spaghetti. We had about ten pounds of ground beef we would have to cook the next day at the latest. Once it was cooked, it would last in the freezer a few more days. Janet and I were doing our best to keep from losing any of the stuff that had previously been frozen. I think we had done a pretty good job.

Russ controlled the dinner conversation. Nothing was left out, even though the boys were with us. His thinking was that they needed to know how serious the situation was, and he was right. They had to know the world was no longer a safe, normal place. It was dangerous and filling up with scumbags. Russ laid out the plan going forward.

"Effective immediately, no one goes outside the house alone. If anyone got caught out when those guys came through, they could have been perceived as a threat, and shot on sight. We are going to have to be vigilant about situational awareness—that means know what is going on around you at all times. Boys, neither of you goes out without a grown-up. Ladies, I'd prefer one of us guys was with you if you go out. Not that I think you can't take care of yourselves, but in the new world that is probably developing out there, you gals have a commodity that would be worth the risk of jumping the fence and grabbing you. For that matter, the boys as well. We just can't take any chances."

Rusty looked at me, then his dad. "What are you talking about, Dad? What 'commodity'? And what does it have to do with me and Ben?"

Russ glanced at me, but it was enough to see me give him a slight shake in the negative. I wasn't ready for this conversation, not now. It wasn't that we hadn't already had "the talk" with Rusty. But that talk didn't involve kidnapping, rape, sex slaves, or anything of that nature that could be spawned in this new rat hole in the making. Russ had a determined look on his face, and I knew he was going to at least touch on the scummier side of this situation.

"Son, there are going to be bad people out there doing bad things to good people. There are probably no cops working, so the bad guys can do all the shit they want to, with no consequences. Look at what they did at the Nelsons'. Broad daylight, and they kick in the back door, break in, and take what they want. Those kinds of people are going to be out, looking for things they can take from other people. Things they can take—or people who can provide something they need. Most of these bad guys won't care if whatever they want to take belongs to someone who doesn't want to give it to them. That includes supplies, shelter, safety, and sex. Do you understand?"

Thank you, baby, for trying to sugar coat it somewhat. I smiled at Russ, and looked to our son. His face was a mixture of disgust and horror—and understanding and anger. Damn whoever caused this. My not-quite-sixteen-year-old son was having to deal with the sordid facts of a lawless existence.

Janet looked frightened as well. Had she not thought about that possibility? From the expression on Bob's face, he had. He looked mad enough to chew up metal and spit out nails. Ben was looking back and forth between his parents, trying to figure out why his mom was scared and his dad was pissed.

Rusty turned to his best friend, saw his confusion, and leaned over to whisper in his ear. Ben's eyes got big, and his face transformed into a younger version of his dad's. Brian was sitting with a concerned, harsh look on his face as well. He didn't have a wife or kid, but he had already adopted us as his own family, and the feeling was mutual. Who would have thought we'd be here, sitting around the table talking about marauders and the things they might do, with a neighbor who last week we barely acknowledged? Things were changing so fast, our world was transforming into a sinister place, and the best we could hope for was to survive until we could get the hell out? Woo frickin' hoo.

Bob stood up. "Well, I think this calls for a shot. No, I'm not saying we get hammered, but I for one could use a good stiff drink. Bourbon, straight up. Who's in? It could be a long night."

Six hands raised at the table. All the grown-ups looked at the kids, who looked back at us with serious expressions. Yeah, they could probably use a little sip as well. I pulled out seven glasses. Bob got the bottle from the liquor cabinet and poured five three-fingers, and two of about one. We each took a glass. Bob was still standing. He raised his glass and took us all in.

"I'd like to propose a toast. To us making it to this point, and to the future we are preparing for. It is not going to be pretty, if what we saw across the street is any indication. But we have each other, and we have each other's backs. We planned for this, and worse. We will get through it, together. Cheers, gang."

We all raised our glasses, clinked them together, and drank the whiskey. The warmth I felt from the tip of my tongue to the pit of my stomach was exactly what I was looking for. Just a few minutes of not thinking about the crap out there.

"Ok, now we'll make some coffee."

Janet was already on her way to the kitchen. We had moved the camp stoves inside, not even in the sunroom anymore. We couldn't take the chance the smell of our food cooking would be picked up on by anybody out scavenging, or the Baxters, for that matter. With the burned-out neighborhood out by the mall, those people would be displaced and looking for somewhere to hole up, maybe even thinking they could ride this out. Since the "visitors" last night, we had brought everything in from the sunroom and the backyard that we had used out there. The less evidence of our existence, the safer we were—for a little while, anyway.

The rest of us stood up with our plates, bowls, glasses, and silverware, and headed to the kitchen. We had a dishwashing station set up at the sinks. Bob directed the boys to dish duty. They grumbled a little, but they got started as soon as Janet dumped some hot water in from the camp stove. The grown-ups got coffee and went back to the table. With what had happened the night before, and then earlier at the Nelson place, sleep would probably not be in abundance. I for one was wired, and I hadn't even had any coffee.

We talked about the ramifications of the scavengers in the area. How long before they started looking in other houses on our street? In our houses? Russ and Bob both felt they would work their way through the houses they could scope out first, like the Nelsons', but eventually they would get to the ones they couldn't see into—and break in to find out what was inside. The longer the power was out, the more desperate people would get. Hell, the Baxters would probably be topping that list in the next day or so. We had a week, maybe two, before they got to our houses. So, the question was, do we leave now, or wait them out?

We talked it over, all the scenarios we could think of—none of them seemed particularly viable, other than the scumbags getting to us sooner or later. So, what was the plan? How could we know the best path to take? For our families, for our future? Where was that crystal ball when you needed it?

# Chapter 11

Since we didn't have a crystal ball, we had to use an alternative plan. The one where we had a 24/7 security detail. The guys manned the watch through the night. During the day, we alternated the boys and us girls. There was always someone watching the front, and half the time someone upstairs watching the road. The guys napped when they could, but we were almost on permanent watch. We cooked inside, trying to use up the rest of the perishable foods that were thawed in the freezer. We cooked the rest of the ground beef and put it back in the freezer with the thawing bottles. We were still maintaining a cool-to-cold temp in there, so the foods we cooked would be good for a few days. The ground beef would be used for spaghetti sauce and shit on a shingle—ground beef in a gravy sauce, on mashed potatoes or bread. We cooked the stew meat, which would give us a few more days before we had to turn it into stew or soup. We were coming down to the final days of the freezer use and were trying to get the most out of the thawing bottles of water.

The next night after the raid on the Nelson house, the pickup was back. It was parked up the street, but the occupants were scoping out the houses on that side of the street—none of those folks had made it back home. Their places were vacant, and thus vulnerable to the scavengers. Well, the upside was they were working that side of the street and not ours—for now. We watched out front and from upstairs. They checked out each house, not breaking into any that we could see. They looked into three more houses on the opposite side of the street. When it looked like they were done, they got back in the truck and left. The rest of the night was quiet.

In the morning, we were eating breakfast—oatmeal, with coffee for the adults and hot chocolate for the boys—when we heard the pickup again. Hearing it during the daylight hours meant there was something worth taking the chance for in one of those houses. Two doors down from the Nelsons'—I didn't know their names— the scavengers pulled into the driveway. Our guys made a beeline for the front windows, with Brian heading up the stairs with Russ's binoculars for the view over the garage. From what they could see, the marauders did the same thing they had done at the Nelsons'. They went around back, then, a few minutes later, they came back out front carrying bags and boxes. We guessed there were at least weapons in the loot they carried out. Why else would they chance being seen in the daytime?

We had no idea how many of them were in the group, where they were staying, or what their plans were. We could guess the plans—take what they needed to survive, by whatever means necessary. As to where they were staying, probably not far. There were other houses between here and the mall, so they could be camped out in there. How many of them there were was the big question. They had taken a bunch of guns—at least half a dozen at the Nelson house, who knew how many at the other place. It sounded like they were arming an ... army? Maybe. Armed mob? Probably. Either way, it was nothing good for us.

We were coming up on a week since the lights went out, and things had to be breaking down, from a societal standpoint. We weren't venturing out past the yard. We needed to get some kind of intel. Time to fire up the mini ham radio.

Russ asked me to go get it from the Faraday cage. I pulled it out and turned it on. Static. But we knew night was better for reception. With the current situation, we didn't have a lot of daytime interference, but even the sun could cause problems. After the sun went down, we should be able to get a clear signal, if there was one out there. That was still a few hours away, so we decided to get back to the business at hand.

Just then, we heard a commotion outside. We beat it back to the windows and saw Dan and Don Baxter standing in their driveway, yelling over to the thieves. Yes, they were that stupid. Could they not see the guns the men had? Could they not figure out what they were doing over there? The Baxter men were asking the scavengers what was going on. Don was belligerent.

"Hey, assholes—what do you think you're doing? That's not your shit. Who do you think you are, just going into people's houses and taking their stuff?"

The guy who seemed to be the leader of the group walked out to the road.

"What business is it of yours, asshole? Is this your house? Mind your business, before I make you my business. Get back in your own house. You don't want to get involved here."

Dan stepped up closer to the road and started yelling over to the men as well. Like father, like son. "Now look here, we know those people. That's Will and Maggie White's house. They must have been at work when everything went off and just haven't gotten back home yet. Probably staying at a hotel or something. You can't just take their things. That's robbery!"

The leader laughed. "Dude, are you clueless or what? If they ain't home by now, they ain't coming home. Everything is off, everywhere. There's no more running water, no more grocery stores, no hotels, no credit cards, no more cars running—well, no new ones—and it's every man for himself. You better be looking after your own—before someone gets to your house and takes what *you* got!" To emphasize his point, he raised the barrel of the shotgun in his hand ever so slightly in their direction.

Dan was looking at the men coming out of the house carrying boxes and bags. From where he was standing, he would be able to see guns, ammo, and food. He had a look on his face like he had just connected the dots—*finally!*—and he leaned over to Don and said something in his ear. Don nodded, and both men backed up, heading backward to their house. Dan was talking as he was backing. "Sorry to bother you, fellas. Y'all have a good day now. We'll be going." The gang leader shook his head and turned back to the Whites' house and his men. "Come on, let's finish this one. We got two more to hit on the way out."

****

Janet and I decided spaghetti would be good for supper, so we got the sauce going. We had canned tomatoes from last summer, as well as dried herbs we had preserved from the herb garden. After it had cooked down, we added the meat and some mushrooms we had gotten on special and dehydrated. Another hour and we'd put the pasta on. Some of Brian's wine would go really well with this meal.

The boys kept watch while the guys got a quick nap. After their latest run, which had included three houses on the other side of the street, the scavengers had left and not come back to the neighborhood. Maybe being confronted by the Baxters would keep them out for a while. Doubtful, but we could hope. The rest of the day was quiet. As the sun was setting, we strained the pasta and called the guys.

Dinner was wonderful. We talked about the group that had been down the street and what they might have gathered from that house. If what they apparently took from the Nelsons' was any indication, it was not a good thing for anybody but them. We also talked about the Baxter clan and the feeling the guys had that we had not heard the last from them. I was sure they were right. Desperate people do crazy, desperate things. I felt bad for the child, but not bad enough to let them get any idea of what we had in the way of supplies. If we gave them anything, they would just keep coming back for more. And I was right—the wine was awesome with the pasta.

After dinner, Janet and I took dish duty, while the guys pulled out the radio. They went out to the sunroom to see if they could get a clear signal. They left the door open so we could hear as well. Russ was scanning channels when we heard a woman's voice come through, clear as day.

*"If anyone can hear this, please let us know where you are. Don't give specifics—just your state, maybe what part. We don't know much more than you do, if you don't know anything. That's pretty much the situation for all of us, that we have heard from. We have gotten reports from north to south, east to west, all four corners, and lots of places in the middle of the country. This is affecting the entire country, possibly the whole continent of North America. We've heard rumors that it was an attack, but not who did it. There has been no statement by any government entity letting us know what's going on or what's being done to fix*

*it, that we have heard. We are going on the assumption that we'll be on our own for a while; there's no telling for how long. Stay tuned to this channel, and we'll provide any updates we get nightly. For now, let's take a few minutes and let you sound off as to where you are. In the meantime, stay strong and vigilant, fellow survivors. God bless us all."*

We sat and listened as people replied with their state and area. We heard middle Tennessee, which got our attention: there were others in our area, possibly similarly prepared, besides us. There truly were people from all over the country commenting, praying, recommending things to do, asking for advice—it got to be almost too much.

The original speaker came back and broke in. *"Okay, sounds like we are getting more and more people on here. We'll try to set up some times for different things to discuss—security, homesteading, first aid, just to name a few that have been brought up. Please tune in tomorrow evening for an attempt at a schedule. Good night, fellow Americans!"*

We had a mixture of feelings. Concern, over how widespread this was. If it affected the whole country, that meant we would be dependent on other countries to help us recover. With all computers and chips in this country fried, replacements would have to come from somewhere else. They would surely want something in return.

Fear, that this could have been an attack. By whom? Who would do something like this? They effectively plunged the majority of this country back to the nineteenth century. The only

131

reason for someone to do something like that is to have the upper hand in a fight. If they had electronics and we didn't, we were dead in the water, army against army. Too much of our military was dependent on electronics.

Anger, at the ones, whoever they were, that had caused all this. The innocent people who had already died, because they didn't have life support, or dialysis, or refrigeration for their insulin, were just the beginning. Most people knew nothing about how to grow food, how to clean game, basic survival knowledge that had been lost in the last hundred or so years—hell, probably just in the last fifty. Those people would likely die of starvation, or be killed by someone they were trying to steal from.

Mostly, we were guardedly optimistic that there were others out there, like us, who were trying to make it as well. We decided we would make every attempt to tune in nightly, to get as much info on the outside world as possible. Things were going to change quickly. The world, at least our part of it, was going to turn into a big steaming pile of dog defecation, and we needed to be as ready for it as we could be.

The guys had brought the chickens and rabbits into the garage, so I wanted to go check on them, to make sure they were good for the night. Russ said he'd go with me. Oh yeah, I forgot—no one goes anywhere alone, and the garage was outside the technical confines of the house. We went to the garage through the door from the kitchen. Russ's truck was inside, and my SUV had been pushed out into the driveway. The truck was much more valuable now. Russ had put up a temp pen for the rabbits, with a dog house for a hutch. The chickens were in cages—cramped, but safe. There was no man door to the outside, so the only other way into the garage was through the garage door or the house. Russ had locked down the big door so no one could open it from outside. They were safe for now.

We were headed back inside when we heard something—or someone—rattling the latch on the gate to the backyard, on the other side of the garage. It was locked from the inside too, but someone was trying to get in. Gee, wonder who that was?

\*\*\*\*

Russ made a beeline for the kitchen and motioned to Bob, and they both headed out the front door. I told Janet and Brian what we'd heard, so Brian headed for the backyard. The boys made to follow him, and I stopped them. Rusty started to complain.

"Mom, we should be out there with Brian, in case someone gets in. He shouldn't be out by himself. What happened to no one goes out alone?"

Smart kid, using our own rules against us.

I conceded, to an extent. "Stay in the sunroom. You can open the windows so you can hear and see, but don't leave the sunroom. Understood?"

I expected a triumphant smirk, but what I got was a serious expression and a curt nod.

"Yes, ma'am. You'll be able to see and hear us the whole time."

I was proud of how grown up he was acting and scared to death that he had to grow up that fast. He and Ben went out to the sunroom, staying back in the shadows and, true to his word, he left the door open to the kitchen.

Janet gave me a tight smile. "I'll stay here, keep an eye on the boys. Why don't you go do the same for the guys?" She knew me so well. I hurried out the front door.

I rounded the corner of the house just in time to see Russ pull his pistol, flip on a Maglite, and yell, "Hold it right there! Hands up if you don't want to get shot!"

The culprit jumped and turned to face him. Yep, Don Baxter. Couldn't even wait forty-eight hours to try to break in. He held his hands up; he was visibly shaking.

"Don't shoot! I didn't take anything! I was just coming to have a look …"

Bob stepped into the flashlight beam. "A look at what? Whatever we have on this property is *none* of your concern and is absolutely *not* yours to take!"

He picked Don up by the front of his sweatshirt and slammed him into the fence. Don grabbed Bob by the wrists, trying to break free, but Bob had him outweighed by half his weight again. Bob was in shape; Don was a skinny little shit. Bob slammed him into the fence again and again, until Don let go of him.

"Look—I'm sorry! We're starving down there. We need food—something, anything!"

Bob let him go. Russ stepped up to Don. "Then I'd suggest you start scavenging in houses people aren't actually living in right now. There should be some things you can grab in some of these empty houses. The one across the street from us has flour, sugar, salt—things those guys you saw today left behind. I hope someone in your house knows how to cook, because you can make food with that stuff. I think all the houses on that side of the street are empty, so I'd suggest you get busy and see what you can find before those assholes come back. If I see you on this property again, you won't get a warning. Now go!" He grabbed Don by the collar and shoved him toward the street.

Don shrugged his shoulders and pulled his sweatshirt back down. His cocky attitude from earlier was gone. He looked at the guys with just a touch of … remorse? Hmmm.

"I'll do that—check those empty houses, I mean. You guys won't see me again, not here. Good luck, fellas." He turned and headed back to his house.

We watched him all the way. Once he had gone inside his own home, we went back into ours. Brian and the boys were coming in the back as well. When we were all together again Russ addressed the group.

"He may be gone for now, but they'll be back. They will ransack the houses down that way and, if they're lucky, get to some supplies before those scavengers. Hopefully, they'll find enough to keep them fed until we get out of here. Guaranteed they'll be through this place once we're gone. For their sake, we better be gone."

****

The night went like the last two. We heard the truck, but it was further down the road, so we couldn't see what houses they were at. That was even better—they were working their way down that side of the street. We didn't know why they had chosen to work one side and not both, but we were counting our blessings for now. Maybe they had seen us out, and knew the house wasn't empty. We weren't careful the first couple of days about being seen. We hadn't thought we needed to be, not that soon. They could have been in the neighborhood though. We weren't really looking for anybody, at least no one that didn't belong in the area. But we also didn't know the folks from the other end of the street, so we wouldn't have known for sure if anyone out there belonged or not.

That's the thing with preppers—we don't get to know "outsiders," because we don't want them to know us, or what we have. We knew our neighbors on either side and the ones directly across the street. The Nelsons were the last house on that side. None of us knew the guy between the Nelsons and the Whites. We thought he worked nights, but we didn't really see him at all. We'd see lights on at different times of the day and night, but only glimpses of him. Kind of creepy, actually.

We maintained the same watch schedule, but this time Rusty stayed up with Brian. He and Ben would alternate nights. Teenage boys still needed a good night's sleep as much as possible. The wives stood watch with their hubbies. We drank coffee, talked, read, and planned. We were trying to decide when we needed to go, to head out for the farm. It hadn't even been a week, but the burned-out neighborhood and the scavengers seemed hell bent on making us bug out sooner than we had planned. That would definitely be the number one topic of discussion tomorrow.

# Chapter 12

Since Russ and I had third watch, I had breakfast ready when everyone got up. We had saved up eggs from the hens for a few days, so I made breakfast burritos. Tortillas can be made with a minimum of ingredients, none of which need refrigeration, so I had a lot of those ingredients on hand. We had dehydrated cheese sauce for when the cheese ran out, which wouldn't take long. Cheese making was not one of my prepping skills. I believe it's an art. I had books on it, but hadn't had access to the whole raw milk we would have at the farm. There was time for that later. For now, we still had shredded cheese in the freezer, some moved there from the fridge, some slowly thawing. When the gang came in, there were smiles all around. Eggs, bacon bits, cheese, tortillas—what's not to love?

We wanted to move the animals out to the backyard for the day, to forage, but it started raining while we were eating. Not that the rain would hurt them, but we decided to wait a bit to see if it stopped. Since we had the trailers pretty much loaded, there wasn't a lot for the boys to do, so I sent them after the tablet in the Faraday cage and told them to take it upstairs and play until it stopped raining. They would be on critter watch when we did take them to the backyard. No more free ranging without a guard, thanks to Don the douchebag. And we would still be bringing them in every night. More work to protect a food source. Thanks a lot, Don.

Rainy day meant indoor work. Janet and I decided to go through the food stores we had in the house, to figure out how long we thought we'd be able to feed everyone without having to break into the stores in the trailers. We were sure we had plenty, but it gave us a chance to gather everything up, to plan out how we would use it. With seven people, there were probably a lot of soups and stews in our future. The guys picked gun cleaning. Ah, the smell of gun oil in the morning.

Even though Janet was a stay-at-home mom, we were both equally skilled in the kitchen. I loved walking in there, looking at what I had on hand, and creating something I hadn't planned. Janet was a recipe gal, while I was more of a "let's throw all this together and see how it turns out" cook. Together, we were amazing. With a few basic ingredients, we could make some awesome meals. I tried to think how it would be to cook when there were no more grocery stores to pop into when you ran out of a particular spice, or flour, or sugar—that was a big one. Spices were easy to stock up on. Most of the time it took just a little to jazz up a dish.

There are quite a few you can grow—sage, thyme, rosemary, basil—so a small herb garden can yield a lot of flavor. Flour is made from wheat, which you can grow as well. Yes, there is some milling involved, but we had grain mills. We could grind wheat, corn, coffee beans, and all with a manual grinder. But sugar was an issue. Sugar comes from sugar cane. Not something you can really grow in Tennessee, since it comes from tropical places. We had hundreds of pounds stored at the farm, but even that would run out someday, if things didn't go back to normal. The alternative was sorghum or honey.

Sorghum we could grow. Honey we had to cultivate, so to speak. We had these things waiting for us at the farm. The sorghum was planted, and the bee hives had been set up a couple of years ago. The colonies were established and thriving. It took a bit to adapt to the difference in taste, so Janet and I were working on ways to incorporate them into our recipes. If a recipe called for a cup of sugar, we substituted one-quarter of a cup of it in honey. We hadn't yet completely replaced honey for sugar in a recipe, but we had subbed up to half. No one knew, or at least they hadn't said anything if they had noticed. Over a cup, we'd need to cut back on the honey, to two-thirds to three-quarters of a cup of honey per one cup sugar, just because honey is so sweet. We'd play that by ear when the time came.

We had pounds and pounds of honey, store-bought, here in town, and Millie had probably just as much stored in the root cellar at the farm. God bless that woman. The sorghum was a larger process, and sorghum has a very distinct flavor, so we didn't have as much of that put back. Monroe had gotten his hands on an old press and a huge pot to cook it down in at an auction. We figured if nothing else, we could use the sorghum, and possibly the honey, as barter items—maybe for sugar! Yeah, we got a good laugh out of that one when I threw it out there. We also had beets planted as a sweetener source. I don't like beets, so I don't know much about them, but Millie swears we can make sugar out of them. I trust Millie, so we planted them. This fall was going to be very educational.

While Janet and I collaborated over cooking, the guys set up on the dining room table with all the handguns. Even though we hadn't had to use them yet, thank goodness, since everybody was carrying they were more exposed to dirt, dust, flour, clothing fuzz, all the things our bodies are around every day. A clean gun is a more reliable gun. That was their motto. Brian was a little embarrassed, because apparently he had just been to the range over the last weekend and hadn't cleaned his pistol when he got back home. You know, the old "I can do that later" excuse we tell ourselves. He had actually planned to do it today, which was Saturday, if nothing else had come up. Bob and Russ gave him a hard time, talking about the shameful condition of his pistol, then laughed, slapped him on the back, and told him not to stress over it. We have all been to the range and not cleaned our guns as soon as we got home.

Bob called up to the boys and told them to bring theirs down. When they came down the stairs and saw what their dads were doing, they immediately wanted to join in. It makes a mom proud to see her son asking his dad to help him strip down his pistol, you know? They pulled up chairs, and soon they were all razzing each other, telling jokes, and laughing together. Janet and I made a big batch of hot chocolate and passed it out to everyone.

With the patter of the rain outside and the laughter inside, it felt almost normal again—except for the kerosene lamps and the camp stove in the kitchen. But then again, this was probably the new normal. I didn't mind. There was a lot less interference. No background noise, like lawn mowers or weed eaters—if anybody was worrying about how their lawn looked right now, they had a lot more problems than they knew—or cars and trucks, air conditioners and fans, transformers—you could hear them hum on quiet nights. I was actually sleeping a lot better since I'd gotten used to the absence of mechanical noise and tuned in to the natural sounds, like wind, rain, crickets, frogs, birds; there were just so many things I hadn't really heard in quite some time. We got a dose of it at the farm, with the windows open, but even there we had fans and a/c, and unless you wanted to get up before dawn, you kept the windows closed, because that damn rooster was going to be crowing like a son of a bitch at the first sign of light in the sky. If we hadn't needed him to make more chickens, I swear I'd have stuck him in a pot. Depending on how hot it got during the summer, that might be a new sound we would have to get accustomed to once we got out there to stay.

By the time the guys had gotten all the guns cleaned, the rain had stopped and the sun was peeking out. I was sure the animals were ready to stretch their legs, so we all went to the garage and grabbed rabbits and chicken cages. We carried them out back, put the rabbits in the big pen, and let the chickens run loose. They'd come to us as soon as we shook some feed in a can at them. We had handled them since they were babies, so there was no problem scooping them up.

We put the boys on animal watch, and Russ and I went to inspect the rabbit pen in the garage. Good thing about rabbit poop, it's easy to clean up. We scooped it into a bag, spread out the straw, and called it good. The chickens were another story. Even with them being in the pens, there were still droppings on the garage floor. We talked it over and decided to throw some water from the rain barrels on it. They were overflowing from the rain that morning anyway. There was a slight downward slope to the garage, so the water would run the droppings to the door. Russ propped it open just enough for the water to run out underneath. With the rain, everything was still wet, so hopefully no one would notice a little extra water running down the driveway.

If we hadn't been close to leaving, we would have captured the chicken poop and saved it to put on some of the plants. Since we weren't staying, there was no reason to save it. We didn't need to take it with us to the farm—there was plenty there as well. We had a great compost pile out there, and since chicken manure is really high in nitrogen, with good amounts of potassium and phosphorus, it is an excellent addition to compost for a garden. Did I say what a font of information Millie and Monroe were?

We had leftover spaghetti for lunch, with a small salad made from the plants in our little garden. I wanted to use what we could before we had to leave. There's nothing like fresh vegetables pulled from your own garden. There was just a little bit of cool left in the freezer, so we were going to have to get what was left in there eaten. Shit on a shingle was on the menu for the evening. That would take care of the last of the ground beef. Beef stew for tomorrow, and we'd be pretty much done with the fresh meats. We had smoked and dehydrated the roasts and tenderloins, and they were all sealed up, most of them in the trailers.

It seemed like it always came down to food. When all the crap was out of the way—jobs, bills, ballgames, TV shows, online surfing—it left eating, sleeping, making sure there was more food to eat, and surviving. Simple, basic, hard, honest work and living. Problem was, there were people out there who didn't plan on hard, honest work to live. They planned to take what other people had worked hard to get. Those guys were assholes, and there were going to be a lot of them out there.

As if to emphasize this, we heard a commotion outside. We headed for the windows front, side, and upstairs. Out front, we saw

Dan and Don Baxter walking out the front door of the Nelson house, carrying grocery bags. It had to be the staples the guys had found there. They put them in a wagon, like I used in the yard, and went to the house next door. We hadn't seen the raiders at that one but we could have missed them, if they had gone through the backyards. They went around back, looking for a kicked-in door apparently. They came back out front in just a minute, empty-handed. The raiders had skipped that one, probably because they couldn't see in. The Baxters, being who they were, didn't want to exert the effort to break in themselves, at least not yet. They wanted the easy haul.

The Whites were next door. They went around back, and in about ten or fifteen minutes were walking out the front with more bags. Apparently they'd gotten over someone taking their neighbors' stuff, as long as it was them. Imagine that.

We couldn't see them out front any further, but Brian was upstairs watching. He let us know they'd hit the next two houses the scavengers had broken into when they kicked in the Whites' back door. From what he could see, they had a wagon full of food stuff. Maybe that would keep them quiet for now. That much food, handled properly, could feed them for at least a week, maybe two, depending on what all they got and how it was prepared. But we doubted they would handle it properly. Their mentality would be similar to the raiders'. If they could get it from someone else, why not?

We all went back downstairs and got ready to batten down the hatches for the evening. Janet and I got busy with the gravy and potatoes. The guys went out back to gather the animals and bring them in for the night. The boys had hosed down the chicken cages while they were out, so between the wet ground and cleaned containers, the chickens and rabbits were pretty clean. They were all put back in the garage, and Russ closed the overhead door all the way.

We made up a batch of iced tea, sweet, of course—we were in Tennessee, after all—and laid out bread for those who wanted theirs that way. Bob would actually put bread on his plate, potatoes on top of that, and the meat and gravy over the whole thing. Actually, that sounded pretty good. I thought I might have mine that way. As everyone got settled, Russ started a conversation.

"We're on close to a week since everything went off. I wasn't expecting things to escalate this fast, but we couldn't have planned for that fire. I think we need to decide when we're going to head out. I don't want us to be here when those scavengers start on this side of the street. I don't want to take the chance on anyone getting hurt. I think tomorrow two of us need to ride the bikes through the woods, back to the main road, and see what it's going to take to get the rigs through there. I wouldn't have a problem with that being me and Brian again, if you're in, Brian."

Brian grinned and nodded. "Sure thing. My legs were burning after our ride the other day, and I forgot how good that felt. I'm in."

Bob looked at Brian, shook his head, and around a bite commented, "Dude, you're sick. No one likes exercise. It just ain't natural."

Brian laughed, and the rest of us joined in. "I've been told that before. I'm working on it."

Bob busted out laughing at that, and Russ continued. "Alright, I'd like us to get out early, hopefully before the assholes that are 'shopping' our street get out and about. We can be out there and back before they get their thieving asses out of bed."

My stomach immediately knotted up. Anytime any of us were away from the group was stressful. I hoped there wouldn't be many of these occasions.

Russ continued. "We need to know if we can get through there without stopping to move vehicles. There's a chance the scavengers have cleared a route for themselves. If they have, and we can get out of this area without many delays, once we get a mile or so past the mall, it should be pretty quiet. One of the reasons the farm worked out so well as our destination is because there aren't many people in that area, including on the way. Once we determine whether or not we have a route, we can decide when we are heading out. I would like that to be in the next day or so. This is the first hurdle before we make that decision."

It was quiet for a few minutes. The question came from Ben. "Uncle Russ, what happens if there isn't a clear path? What do we do then?"

Russ looked at him with a small smile. "One thing at a time, Ben. We need to check it first. Then we'll decide what to do next."

We checked in on the radio that night. There were transmissions with info about first aid, security, homesteading, and a lot of questions about what had happened to put us in this situation. Lots of questions that no one had answers to. And where was the "government" in all this? No one on the air had seen any sign of anyone official. But then again, did we really want that?

****

The scout team for the scavengers showed up that night—at Brian's house. It was just after midnight, so good and dark. Brian got up the stairs as fast as he could and woke everybody up. We quickly put on shoes and armed ourselves. If they were starting on this side of the street, we needed to be ready. The scouts hadn't broken in anywhere that we knew of, and they hadn't marked any houses for the scavengers that they couldn't see into. But who knew if they would keep to that method? We wanted to know what they were doing. Russ grabbed the night vision monocular and went to the window on that end of the house, at the top of the stairs. He watched the scouts go around to each window they could reach in the front. Since Brian had a privacy fence like we did, and it was locked, they couldn't easily get to the back of the house. Maybe that would make them skip his house. Not that there was anything of use to them over there, but just the thought of some jerkwads going through your house—Brian was seething, and I could totally understand why. I'd feel exactly the same way.

Brian was antsy, pacing back and forth in front of the window. "I can jump the fence into my yard, go out the gate and kick their asses. What right do they have to be on my property?"

Bob tried to talk him down. "Bubba, I know how you feel. If it was my place, I'd feel the same way. In fact, if they work their way over there, you may be the one holding me back. But we need to lay low as long as possible. While it might deter them if they find people in a house, it may also give them the idea that, because there are people at home, there's a good chance they have food, guns, water—the stuff they're after. We have a plan, long term: past next week, past next month, hell past next year. We have to get out of here to do that. We want to get out of here with the trucks and trailers, but we're getting to the farm, one way or the other. We can't get there if we're hurt or dead. You know what I mean?"

Brian stopped, took a deep breath, and nodded. "I'm sorry, man. It just pisses me off to see them traipsing around my house like they have some right to do it. But, it's cool. We'll watch and see what they do."

149

A short while later, the strangers left Brian's place and walked across the yard—to our house. Here we go.

# Chapter 13

Your home is your castle: your safe place, your haven, your escape from the world. When you're at home, you're comfortable and secure. At least that's the way it should be. In this situation, there was no security, no safety. We were at the mercy of circumstances beyond our control and people with no morals. And one of the most violating feelings is someone in your home who is not invited, or is not supposed to be there. No, they weren't in our house, but they were outside, trying to see in, and that was close enough.

We stayed upstairs, so that there was no chance they might see us moving around if they were looking in. Not that they could see in, but you never know, so why take the chance? We stayed as still as possible, barely breathing. We tried to listen to what they were saying to each other, but they were talking in a low voice, just loud enough to hear each other.

After about ten minutes, we heard them moving away, toward Bob and Janet's. Their place was closed up as tight as ours and Brian's, so hopefully they would leave it alone as well. The next one down was the Baxters', and they were just too ignorant to stay inside.

Dan popped open the front door, shined a flashlight at them, and yelled, "What are you doing here? Get the hell off my lawn! We've got guns! My boy is in there with you in his sights!"

Good Lord, he'd told them he had guns. We hadn't really thought they did after the remarks they had made the other day, but they could have had something, like a .22, or a shotgun. If Don was really dealing drugs, like we thought, he may have had something more substantial.

The scouts took a step back but didn't run or anything. They looked at Dan and said something we couldn't hear. They weren't yelling, like Dan had been. They started backing away, out to the road, coming back down the street toward us. They kept their eyes on Dan as they walked backward, talking to each other. They had left their truck at the end of the street just past Brian's house. They got in and headed out of the neighborhood. Hopefully they would consider the night a bust. I prayed they would.

By the time they had gone, it was close to 2:00 a.m. We still had about four hours until sunrise. It was Bob and Janet's watch for a couple more hours, so the rest of us headed off to bed to try to get a few more hours' sleep. Not sure if that was going to happen, but we had to try. The next day could prove to be a very busy one. The thing we'd been expecting since they had shown up in the neighborhood, and dreading, was here. They had been to our house. How long before they broke in to see what we had locked up so tight?

****

Russ managed to get three more hours of sleep. Bob let him sleep a bit longer, since he and Brian were heading out early to check the road and the area. I got up with Russ, as planned, and we kept it quiet so Brian could sleep in the den. At 7:00, he woke Brian up. I had pancakes and coffee ready for them. Coffee by itself would get Bob and Janet up, and it did. When they found out there were pancakes, I got hugs from both of them.

Russ and Brian finished eating, brushed and flossed—without being reminded—and grabbed their bags. Since they hadn't used anything but a bottle of water each the last time they went out, that was all they had to add back. They grabbed their sidearms, a two-way radio, their bags, and coats—it was looking like rain again. That could be a good thing; most of the time, scavengers and raiders were like animals, and they would hole up when the weather was bad. Ironic, the similarity to animals. It was possible that if it rained, it would be safer for them out there in the woods.

I hugged and kissed Russ, and hugged Brian as well.

"Be safe. Hurry back."

They both smiled and went to the garage. Bob went out front, checked for anyone out and about, and came back in.

"All clear, fellas. Just go out the front door so we don't have to open the garage door. Call us on the radio if anything happens. I'll be there in a flash, in the truck, scavengers be damned."

Man hugs occurred, and they headed out. I closed my eyes, said another prayer, and went back to the kitchen to whip up more pancakes for the boys. Bob followed me in.

"You know, Annie, I wouldn't mind another short stack of those myself."

I smiled at my brother-in-love, gave him a peck on the cheek, and ruffled his hair.

"You've got it, hun. Go get the boys up. They'll be ready when you get back down."

Because that was what I needed to do: stay busy. If I stopped long enough to think about Russ being out there with those dirtbags, wherever they were hanging out, it could drive me bonkers. I needed to work on something to take my mind off the situation. I decided to try to do some laundry.

I had bought this manual washing machine. I use the term "machine" loosely, because it was not a machine. It was kind of a tub, with a lid, and a crank handle on the side. You put the clothes in, added water and a little detergent, and turned the crank. It wasn't my Kenmore, but beggars can't be choosers when the electronic age is suddenly brought to a halt. I had a wash tub with clean water to rinse in. When one batch came out, I put another in. Janet found me in the laundry room and took over the rinsing.

Once that was done, she wrung the clothes out and hung them on the rack in the corner. Since it looked like rain, we didn't want to hang them outside. We washed and rinsed until the rack was full. If we hadn't been trying to keep a low profile, we could have started a fire and used the warmth to dry them faster, but after last night, we didn't want to take the chance anyone would see the smoke. We hoped the rain wouldn't last long; then we could hang some more outside.

With as much laundry done as we had room to hang, I didn't have anything to keep me occupied. Janet led me to the table, set a cup of coffee in front of me, and surprised me with one of the e-readers. She opened it up, clicked it on, and looked at me.

"Let's learn how to make jam."

I smiled and nodded at her. That should keep my mind occupied. My best friend was a genius. Now, if only the lesson would keep my mind off what might be going on with Russ and Brian.

# Chapter 14

Brian led them through the woods on the same route they had traveled earlier. The closer they got to the highway, the more evidence there was that other people had been in the woods, and not too long ago. Most of the prints and trash were close to the highway, not back toward the houses, so it was possibly still somewhat safe from scavenging bands. Not that anyone could blame them. Without being prepared for something like this, the group would be in the same position, trying to figure out how to feed everyone. And yet, from an informed viewpoint, these tragic, and probably desperate, people would be seen as predators and potential raiders, after precious supplies. Vigilance was the new byword.

When they got close to the spot where they would be able to see the road, Russ called softly to Brian.

"Let's get off and walk from here. We can hide the bikes off the path right over there. I don't want to take a chance of getting ambushed and losing them."

Brian headed off the path to the spot Russ had indicated. It was bushed out with spring leaves, and there were dead branches lying close by. They put the bikes in a thicket and laid branches over them. They backed up to the path, looking at the camouflage. They couldn't see anything that looked suspicious, and they were peering in, trying to see them. Satisfied with their work, they grabbed their bags and headed for the road on foot.

The closer they got, the more they could see that everything was not the same as it had been when they came through a few days ago. There seemed to be a definitive path down the road. Apparently, the scavengers had cleared themselves a route in and out of the area. Cars were pushed off to the sides of the road. Good thing—the less time it took to get out of there, the sooner the arrival at the farm, and the safer the trip getting there might be. The downside was that they could have sentries set up, watching for people trying to get out of the area. There could be roadblocks, snipers, all sorts of assault points.

Russ wanted to parallel the road for a while to the south and see what else they could see. He pulled out his binoculars and scanned the area.

"I don't see anybody, but that doesn't mean there's not anybody there. Keep your eyes open and try to listen for anything out of the norm. Stay in the woods so we can stay out of sight as much as possible."

Brian headed south on the path. Russ took another quick, magnified look, and followed him. They were constantly scanning the road, as well as the sides, looking for any movement, or any sign that someone had recently been around. It was still early, probably around 8:00, so it was possible there weren't a lot of people up yet. Funny thing about when SHTF—if no one had a "job" to go to, most people didn't think it mattered what time you got up. Those who were ready for this new world—or as ready as modern-day folks could be—knew there were still things that needed to be done, so if no one else was up early, imagine the things you could get to first: deer, squirrels, rabbits; wild edible plants and berries; wild game birds and their eggs. The old saying "the early bird gets the worm" depicted this new world to a T. Maybe even more relevant was the saying "You snooze, you lose." This was not the time to be catching up on sleep. This was when, if you didn't have supplies, you became a hunter-gatherer, like cavemen, native Americans, or any of the people who existed before grocery stores and planted gardens, before houses and huts. Though there were houses now, they would be more like huts, except for having real floors instead of dirt. No electricity or running water reduced houses to shelters. Sleeping in probably wasn't the best idea right now for Joe Citizen, but their laziness was working at the moment.

As they walked the edge of the woods, Russ and Brian tried to keep an eye out for people, but also tried to note what had changed since they had gone through the area before. They were now seeing a difference. Different vehicles, abandoned for a week now, but in the same condition as the ones in the other direction—windows broken, doors and trunks left open, nothing of value left anymore.

They had been pushed to the side, some into the ditch, to clear a lane on the road. Most looked like they had been pushed with a large vehicle, no care taken, as there were dents, smashed fenders and quarter panels—who would care? These vehicles were most likely sitting in the place they would be for a very long time, maybe forever. They were worthless now. Even if the chips could be replaced, by the time the cars were taken apart to do it, new ones could probably be built, cheaper and in less time, if the factories were able to start back up again. No, these cars and trucks had no value anymore.

Brian paused, looked back at Russ, and pointed ahead toward the road. When Russ pulled out his binoculars and checked, he saw what looked to be a family walking down the road away from them—a man, a woman, and two young girls, pushing a shopping cart and pulling a wagon, both containing bags Russ couldn't see into, as well as some clothes, blankets, and other things they couldn't make out. Russ shook his head and spoke to Brian in a low voice.

"You see the mistakes they're making?"

No time like the present to continue Brian's education of the way things were now. Brian looked at them again and started his recitation.

"First and biggest one that I see is walking the road, out in the open. They obviously have supplies of some kind, or else what would they be hauling in the wagon and cart? They have no cover, so if someone comes at them, they have no chance of hiding."

He looked at Russ, who nodded. Brian continued. "They have supplies in grocery bags, so a good chance it's food. It's ingrained in us to put groceries in grocery bags. That would make it worth taking their stuff right off the bat. The wife and girls are a valuable resource, and it is very easy to see that's what they are. They aren't hiding their hair, form, anything."

Russ spoke up then. "Knowing all that, say you're a piece-of-shit scumbag and you see them on the road. What do you do?"

Brian shook his head. "Kill the dad. The mom freaks out, screaming and grabbing her kids. Now all three are in one nice little bundle. Swoop in, grab the mom and the girls, the cart and the wagon, load them up in a truck, and haul them off. Five minutes, tops."

"Good assessment, and probably pretty accurate. It sucks that we have to think like them, but it sucks even more that people like that don't. Let's go. Maybe we can save a life or four today."

Russ moved toward the family at a faster pace, while still staying within the relative cover of the woods. When they were almost abreast of them—and not surprisingly, the family still didn't know they were there—Russ whistled, softly, like calling a dog. The man and woman both looked up and in their direction. Russ stepped just to the edge of the woods, with his hands out to the side showing they were empty, and motioned for the small family to come toward him. The father held his arm in front of his family and pulled a small revolver out of his pocket. Well, at least they had a weapon, so to speak. Not much good if someone shoots you in the head from a hundred yards with a rifle though. Russ looked the father in the eye.

"If we wanted to kill you, you'd be dead. We've been following you for five minutes. I'd like to help you and your family survive for a little while longer. Please come over and talk to us. My name is Russ Mathews. This is my friend, Brian Riggins. Please come over, away from the road. You are out in the open and could be attacked easily."

The man and woman both immediately looked around, trying to take in every direction, and seemed to see what Russ was trying to tell them. The dad spoke softly to his wife, who grabbed her daughters by the hand, and they all headed toward Russ and Brian. That was a good start.

When the small family got to the edge of the woods, the man pocketed the 38 Special—easy to see what it was up close—and held his hand out to Russ.

"Sean Scanlin. This is my wife, Kate, and our daughters, Tara and Katlyn. Are you guys from the Woodlawn Plantation houses up there?"

Sean motioned with his head back toward the burned-out neighborhood up by the mall. Russ shook his head. Sean kept talking.

"We lived on Walton Lane. The whole area is gone. We waited for the fires to burn out. The rain yesterday helped. There wasn't much left, but we found a few basements that were not completely burned out. We grabbed what we thought we might possibly be able to use and headed out. We have some friends who live about twenty-five or thirty miles from here. That's the best option we could come up with. We figured we could walk there in a week. We didn't know what else to do. Nothing is working, everything is gone, there's no food, no water, now no shelter. We just hoped we could make it to our friends' place. They have a small farm, and know all about gardening, and they raise goats and chickens and stuff. Sorry, I'm rambling. Where are you guys from? Do you have a camp or something nearby?"

Brian looked to Russ, who shook his head. "No, we don't have anything close. We are out scouting for a route out of here. It's going to get bad anywhere there are houses around that might have supplies. I just wanted to talk to you about how you were traveling, out in the open like that. You need to be traveling in the woods. It will take you longer to get where you're going, but it will at least provide you some cover. This path will follow the highway for quite a while, right, Brian?"

Brian nodded, and Russ continued. "Your family is in real danger. Your wife and daughters will be a high commodity in the lawless world that's brewing as we speak. You need to keep them hidden as much as possible. You seem to have some kind of supplies. I would consolidate everything into one place—either the cart or the wagon. Make it look like less. Cover the whole thing with a blanket, with clothing showing under it, so it looks like clothes instead of food. Cut your daughters' hair, short, so they look like boys, or tuck it up under a hat or cap. Hide your wife under a coat or a poncho. When you absolutely have to leave the cover of the woods, check the area first. Check for other people. Don't trust anybody. You shouldn't have trusted us, but I'm glad you did. When you stop to sleep, post a guard. You and your wife will need to trade off. Move deep into the woods to make camp. No fires during the day. Night is safer, but keep it small. I hope you have ammo for that revolver, and I really hope you have some other guns. Don't share info with anyone you don't know about what you have. People will kill you for your food or weapons soon. The main thing you need to keep in the front of your mind is be invisible. You don't want anyone to see or hear you. Understand?"

Sean was clearly trying to absorb everything Russ was saying. Kate had a lost look. She looked at Russ with a question in her eyes. "Why are you doing this? Why are you trying to help us? You didn't have to let us know you were here. You could have kept going, and we would have been none the wiser."

Russ returned her look. "I have a son. If I didn't know what I know, I would hope someone would help me so he could live."

Sean's head snapped up. "You know something? You know what happened? Why nothing works?"

163

Russ shook his head again. "I don't know for a hundred percent proof positive. I do have a theory. I think it was an EMP, an electromagnetic pulse. A nuclear weapon detonated in the atmosphere can cause the pulse, or even a large solar flare, which takes out anything electronic with computer chips. It's like sticking them in a microwave. They're fried. I don't know who did it. I don't know why. I know if that's what it was, it will be a long time before we have any semblance of normalcy in our world. I know that with no police, the bad guys are going to be running rampant. I know that the good, decent people will need to band together if they are going to make it and have a fighting chance at survival. Are you good people?"

Sean and Kate looked at each other. Sean spoke up. "We are good people. We just want to keep our kids safe. Can you help us? Can we join you? We don't have a lot, but we have some food we could share. What can we do to get you to consider taking us with you?"

Brian looked at Russ with a question in his eye. Russ shook his head. "Right now, we are out here scoping out an exit route. Our neighborhood is being cased by scavengers, possibly marauders, so we are getting ready to leave. We will probably be through here tomorrow, or the next day at the latest. The best I can offer you is this: keep heading south. Stay to the woods. We'll be watching this side of the road on our way out. Watch for two rigs—a pickup and a big SUV, both hauling white trailers. If you're out here and you see us, flag us down. If you've made it that long, we'll pick you up and give you a ride down the road, maybe pretty close to where you're headed. Can you work with that?"

Sean smiled and nodded. "Yes, we can work with that. Thank you, Russ. You're a good man. Are you guys going this way? Can we walk with you for a while?"

Russ smiled at him. "Yes, we're still checking the area out, so you can tag along."

They walked the path through the woods, with Russ and Brian leading the way, Sean and Kate behind with their kids and their belongings. Russ shared with them what they'd heard on the radio and what had happened on the street. Sean and Kate told the story of the horrible fire that took out their home.

"Someone—no one ever admitted to it—accidentally set their house on fire, trying to cook inside," Sean said. "It went up fast, then the wind came in, and with no firefighters, we had no way to control it. It was dark, and by the time we smelled the smoke, the whole end of the street was blazing. We grabbed the kids and ran out. The street burned all night, and there were dozens of people standing around, wondering what to do next. We had heard gunshots coming from the mall area the last couple of nights, so we didn't want to go anywhere near there. I had my .38 revolver and a nine-millimeter pistol in my coat pockets when we ran out of the house, thank goodness. Once the gunshots started, I made sure to always have them on me. I got Kate and the girls, and we headed to the edge of the neighborhood. There was a park, with a playground and a playhouse. We moved in and closed it up. We spent the rest of the night listening to the people out there trying to figure out what to do, where to go. We heard a couple outside the playhouse, but we had secured the door with a huge rock inside, so they probably thought it was locked at night. The next morning, we peeked out and saw a lot less people, and the complete devastation of our homes. Kate fell apart, the girls cried, and I tried to figure out what to do next."

Russ and Brian had been splitting their attention between the surrounding area and Sean's tale. They couldn't hide the sympathy in their eyes for the great loss this family had been through. Sean went on.

"I decided to leave Kate and the girls in the playhouse so I could scout for supplies, and I gave Kate my nine-millimeter. I had taught her how to handle a gun and how to shoot. She wasn't as comfortable with it as I was, but she could defend the girls. The smoke was still really thick, so visibility was very low, which actually worked in my favor. I found a wagon and went around the edge of the burned houses and the very outside edges of the mall. There wasn't much, but little things can help a lot. A tin of tuna, a half-jar of peanut butter, a sleeve of crackers—anything that could even remotely be considered food, I grabbed. I checked cars in the back of the mall parking lot, too. And that's where I scored. There was a car sitting in the middle of an area, you know, like it stopped right when the shit went down."

Kate cleared her throat. Sean laughed. "Sorry, sweetie. It's been a rough morning. Sorry girls."

The girls giggled, the first sound the guys had heard from them. Sean went on. "Apparently, whoever had been driving it had just been to the grocery store. When the car died, they must have just left and started walking home. The door wasn't even locked—probably didn't remember the electronic door lock wasn't working when they tried to use it. I opened the driver's door and popped the trunk latch. Thank goodness it wasn't electrical. The trunk had half a dozen bags of food. It smelled really bad—there was spoiled meat in a thermal bag, but fortunately it was separate from the other stuff. There was bread, crackers, Vienna sausages, peanut butter, chips, all kinds of food stuff, as well as juice boxes and a couple of cases of bottled water. I looked around, didn't see anybody watching, and grabbed everything that didn't stink and loaded it in the wagon, bags and all. With the other things, the wagon was pretty full, and I was afraid someone was going to see what I had, so I took my coat off and threw it over the top.

"I kept to the edges and worked my way back to the playground. As I was walking up, I saw a woman and two kids walking through the park. She saw me and rushed over. She asked me for some food for her kids. I looked at the kids and couldn't turn my back on them. I went to the wagon and pulled out the half-jar of peanut butter and a sleeve of crackers and handed them over. She took them, thanked me, and hurried away.

"I went on to the playhouse and called out to Kate to let her know it was me. She opened the door, and I pushed the wagon in. It was kind of cramped, but we needed to keep the food with us. The girls asked for something to eat. It was past noon and we hadn't eaten since the evening before. Kate grabbed a few things from the wagon and fed us all. While we were eating, I heard someone outside. Close. I motioned to the girls to be quiet, and we listened. I could hear the woman I had given the food to, talking to a man. She told him about seeing me with the wagon. They were trying to figure out where we were. They tried the door on the playhouse, but again the rock must have given the appearance it was locked. In a few minutes, they moved away. I knew then we had to leave. I whispered to Kate my plan to go to Luke and Casey, our friends in the country. We decided to wait until dark and head out."

Sean paused, like he didn't really want to talk anymore, or didn't want to tell the next part. Russ and Brian waited patiently. If he needed to tell them he would; if not, their story would end there, as far as the guys were concerned.

They were definitely getting an idea of what had happened when the neighborhood burned. They felt bad for the Scanlins, as well as the other families who had lost their homes that night. Just when they thought he wouldn't continue, he did.

"About an hour after sunset, I opened the door and took a look outside. I didn't see anybody, so I had the girls come out and bring the wagon. We headed for the back side of the mall, giving it a wide berth, so we could get to the highway. I figured we could follow it south, which was the way to the country. As soon as we got to the edge of the park, someone called out from the dark. It was the woman again, but she looked to be alone this time. She said she needed some more food for her kids, that what I had given her earlier was gone. I told her I couldn't spare any more, since I had my own kids to feed. Just then, a man stepped out behind her with a baseball bat. He said he was 'real sorry' about my kids, but they needed to feed theirs too. He said to hand over the wagon and no one would get hurt. His wife—at least, I guessed that was what she was—pulled out a grocery cart that had some blankets and coats and stuff in it—mostly clothes. Her man came toward me, swinging the bat like he was warming up for his at-bat.

"When he was about ten feet away, Kate and I both pulled out our guns. I pointed mine at him, and Kate pointed hers at the woman. They both stopped, wide-eyed. I told him to drop the bat and kick it over to me. He did as he was told, but he wasn't happy about it. Kate told the woman to push the cart over as well. She started to protest, saying it was all they had and how could we take it. Kate said, 'The same way you were about to take ours.' It was pretty bad ass."

They all laughed as Kate blushed.

"We took the cart, grabbed the wagon, and headed out. Oh, and we took the bat, too. We've been walking ever since."

Brian asked, "How did you keep them from following you? I would think that as soon as you turned your back on them, they would have been on you immediately."

Kate spoke up then. "They had some really good stuff in their cart. Rope, duct tape. Sean wrapped them up inside the playhouse, taped their mouths shut, and closed the door."

She smiled at her husband. He grinned back at her. So, they were survivors after all. They just needed some guidance.

By now, they had gotten to the next exit off the highway. Russ held up his hand to get everyone to stop and wait. He checked the area with the binoculars. He paid particular attention to the underpass—the perfect spot for an ambush. When he didn't see any threats, he turned back to the group.

"This is as far as we go today. I think if we can get this far with the rigs, we should be in good shape. We haven't been in the woods on the other side, but I think if you stick to the woods, you'll be a lot safer. Try to stay close to the highway, just not too close. Like I said, we'll be through here in the next few days. Keep an eye out. We'll be looking for you from this point on, for the next fifteen or so miles. I doubt you could get much further than that with the little ones. Are you okay with food and water? How about ammo?"

Sean pulled his pistol out. "I think we'll be okay with food and water. As far as ammo, we have what's in the guns. I wasn't carrying any spare on me, just the guns."

The pistol had a fifteen-round magazine. Russ pulled out his bag and dug to the bottom. He fished out a box of target ammo and handed it to Sean.

"This is for my wife's gun. I try to carry a spare box of each of our caliber, as well as the magazines. Take it. We have more at home."

Sean took the box. "Thank you, Russ. You guys are awesome. I hope we see you again, soon." He held his hand out to Russ, who shook it, and held on for a moment longer.

"Don't forget what I said about the girls. Hide the fact that they're female. That's your number one priority. Good luck, Sean."

Brian reached out and shook Sean's hand as well. "You guys head on out. We'll cover you, make sure you get across the street to the woods on the other side. If you see anything shady, holler."

Sean nodded and grabbed one of his girls' hand, Kate grabbed the other's, and they headed out. The guys watched them all the way. At the edge of the woods on the other side, they transferred everything to the wagon, ditched the grocery cart, and, with a wave, headed into the woods. The fellas wished them well and good luck. They'd probably need it.

# Chapter 15

Without the distraction of the conversation, Russ and Brian paid a bit better attention on the way back. They noticed that not too far from the mall the cars thinned out on the road headed south. Since it was very rural in that direction, it made sense. Even the people who lived out that way would have been heading north, if they had to go to work in town. This was going to work out very well for the journey. Once past the mall, which had already been cleared to an extent, there shouldn't be any issues.

Since they hadn't seen any bad guys so far, they were also thinking this time of day would be a good time to travel. Of course, they had kept themselves hidden in the woods and had not been out on the road. There could still be problem people out there, but maybe the group could out run them. Hopefully. They made their way back to where they had stashed the bikes. Everything was as they had left it. After checking the area, they pulled the bikes out and turned back toward the house.

They had barely gotten back on the trail when they heard the truck. Reflex made them jump off the bikes and work their way deeper in the brush. They could see the road leading away from the burned-out neighborhood and the mall, and the truck was on it, heading toward their home. There were a few other streets out that way, so there was a chance it wasn't necessarily going to theirs. Since they'd been regular visitors the last few days and nights, probably not a really big chance. Make that fat chance.

The truck followed the road and went around a curve, so the guys couldn't see it anymore. They mounted up and took off. If those assholes were headed to our street, our place, they wanted to be there. Brian told Russ he knew a path deeper in the woods that would get them home faster. Since they didn't really care anymore about watching the road, Russ told him to lead the way. Brian took the left fork at the next break in the path, and they put the pedal to the metal, so to speak. They dodged limbs and trees, and scared up rabbits, squirrels, and a wild turkey. That one scared the shit out of them; those things make a hell of a noise trying to take flight. Brian almost wiped out on a boulder. It would have been funny if they hadn't been on a mission to get home as fast as possible.

They got to the edge of the woods behind the house and stopped. Russ pulled up his binoculars and checked the area. He wasn't able to see in front of the houses, but he had a line of sight between them. It looked clear, and he didn't hear the truck, or anyone out and about. They decided to leave the bikes in the woods for now, so they could check things out before they headed in. They made a dash for the fence behind the house and pulled their sidearms. Russ motioned that he would go to the corner on the right, and for Brian to go toward his place in the other direction. Brian nodded and took off.

Russ got to the corner and looked around the edge of the fence. It looked clear, and he didn't hear anything, but he stayed low anyway. He crept up the side of the fence and stopped at the front corner. He could hear men talking, and they weren't really trying to be quiet. It sounded like it was coming from Bob and Janet's front yard.

"Can you see inside, Joe? Seems like the ones on this side of the road are closed up tighter than a virgin's legs."

Russ heard at least two men laugh at the crude remark. "Nah, all three of these down to the end I can't see nothin' inside. We can try bustin' into one of 'em, see if there's anyone, or anything, inside. That one on the end and this one next to us both have a big fence. We could jump it, have some cover for kickin' in the back door. Hell, we can go in the front if you want. Ain't seen nobody on this street except them dumbasses next to this one. I don't reckon they'd cause us any trouble. That old man about pissed hisself the other day when Les told him to fuck off. I bet they ain't even got no guns in there. Just struttin' around like a peacock, tryin' to impress somebody."

The original speaker—Russ hadn't heard his name—spoke again. "Let's go talk to Les, see what he thinks."

He heard the men head back toward the road. Apparently the truck was in front of Bob and Janet's house. Russ backed up, keeping his eye out front, and feeling his way back behind the fence. He turned the corner and saw Brian heading toward him. Russ motioned for him to stay and went over to him. He told Brian what he heard.

"Do you think we should make our presence known? Do you think it would get them to move on, maybe to the next road down?"

Brian nodded. "You know, we can jump the fence to my house, get in and walk out the front door, like that's where we're staying. That will take their focus off this house and maybe get them to move on. I have a key hidden in the backyard. What do you think?"

Russ grinned. "That's a great idea. Let's go."

They ran to Brian's section of the fence, and Russ gave Brian a leg up. Brian climbed up, looked over the edge of the fence to see if anyone was looking, or could see him, then straddled the fence at the top. He reached back down to help Russ. They jumped down into Brian's backyard, and Brian headed to his outdoor kitchen, knelt down, and pulled a specific brick out of the back. It came out with mortar attached on all the edges. In place, you couldn't tell it was loose.

"Sweet hide-a-key, bubba. Taking a mental note to remember that one," Russ said.

A key was taped on the back of the brick. Brian pulled it off and headed to the back door. He opened it, but stopped and pulled his pistol out before he went in. The thugs could have already decided to come in. He looked into his kitchen, through to the living room. It was clear. He gave Russ a curt nod and headed in; Russ already had his gun out. They went to the front door and saw it was still locked. They holstered their weapons and got their plan worked out.

"We go out, sidearms holstered but openly visible. Don't say anything first—let them start the conversation, if there is one. Just go out front and look their way. If they say something, we'll respond. If they don't say anything, but don't make a move to leave, I'll engage them. Let's go. I don't want to give them time to decide to bust into our place."

Brian unlocked the door and they went out. Time to meet the shit birds.

****

Les was sitting in the truck, smoking a joint. Not like he had to hide it—no one had seen a cop in a week. This street had been pretty good for gathering supplies. That house across the street didn't have much for food, but damn that boy had guns. The one two doors down had lots of food, probably old people. His grandma always had food at her house. The rest of the houses to the end on that side had yielded a nice pile of food, weapons, and, one in particular, drugs. They could lay low for at least a month on the food they had grabbed. They could stay high that long, too, if they wanted to. Les was smart though—he knew the new "money" was everything they had been grabbing up. There was quite a bit of microwave food, and they still had to figure out how to cook that without a microwave—maybe they'd trade that for something else. Let someone else figure out how to cook it without electricity.

His crew consisted of Joe and Mac, out there scouting more houses, and Ray, Junior, and Dave back at the stash. They had set up in one of the small shops at the mall, after they boarded up the front. Who would come in looking for anything in a boarded-up storefront? They had started in a storage unit on the other side of the mall. It still had some stuff in it, so they kept it locked and checked it every day. It was mostly the microwave food, so not a big loss if it got stolen. The shop was a much better location, since it had a lot of space, shelves they could sort the stuff out on, and with the front boarded up, just a man door coming in or out.

So far, they hadn't had to take anybody out. That was why they were working the empty houses first. There were lots of cars on the road, some with plates from the next county down, so they figured lots of people got caught away from home. Those houses were easy to clean out. If the owners weren't home yet, most likely they wouldn't be, ever. Les was trying to keep this low key for as long as possible. He knew it would get bloody at some point, so right now he was getting what he could with the least amount of trouble. If this side of the street wasn't open, he was just going to get the boys loaded up and head over to the next street. No sense taking chances yet, if they didn't need to. There could be some whack job barricaded in one of those places waiting to ambush them. They didn't have to put themselves in a position like that at this point.

Joe and Mac were heading toward him now, but as Les started to call out to them he saw two guys behind them at the house on the end. They were standing there looking down the road toward his truck. And they had guns on them. Shit! He leaned out and yelled, "Behind you, idiots!"

They both turned and saw the two men standing there. They stopped, but didn't leave. Les got out of the truck and joined them on the lawn a couple of houses down. Together, they started toward the guys. Eventually, one of the men spoke up.

"Can we help you boys?"

Les smiled at him. "Just checking the area for supplies. Stores are empty, ya know? Didn't want any trouble, man. We check to make sure the house is empty first, so we don't take someone else's stuff, you know?"

The man nodded. "Yeah, I know, but just because someone isn't home, doesn't mean they won't be. What happens if they make it home, and you took all their supplies? How do they eat, feed their kids? What right do you have to take other people's things?"

The dude was getting fired up. Les took a defensive stance. "Hey man, we ain't hurtin' nobody. You know as sure as we do that if they ain't home by now, they probably ain't gettin' home. Someone's going to get this stuff sometime. It might as well be us. We didn't know anybody was on this street, except those assholes over there."

He motioned with his head back to the house further down the street. As he turned to look, he saw another man coming out of the house of the lawn they were standing on, with a pistol holstered and a shotgun in his hands. He exchanged a nod with the guy Les had been talking to.

Les quickly figured out they were evenly matched, maybe even in a deficit, and they were covered front and back. The two strangers both had their hands resting on their pistols.

The newcomer spoke up. "I think you boys should get in your truck and move on. You've done all the shopping you're going to do on this street. You get me?"

Les looked at all three men and slowly nodded. He motioned to Joe and Mac.

"Yeah, we'll be movin' on now. You fellas have a good day now, ya hear?"

They backed away, keeping the men in their line of sight, but making no moves for their weapons. They loaded up, turned around, and left the neighborhood. They didn't look back.

***

Bob walked over and met Russ and Brian in the yard. He grinned at them.

"You guys didn't think I was gonna let you have all the fun, did you?"

Russ slapped him on the back. "Nice situational awareness, brother. Thanks for the backup. Let's get these houses locked down again, and get a meeting going ASAP. Unless something changes, we head out in the morning. First thing."

# Chapter 16

Once the guys got the other two houses locked down, they came back in. Russ and Brian shared the story of their trip with us, including meeting the Scanlins. My heart broke for that young family. I could imagine how I would feel if we didn't have the supplies we had and everything went down. Thank goodness Russ got through to me and we were prepared. Things would be a whole lot different if he hadn't. We'd be out scavenging, looting—let's call a spade a spade: stealing other people's stuff—to feed our families, just like the raiders from earlier, just like the Scanlins. Food and water are basic life necessities. No food and water, no life. What would you do, what lengths would you go to, so you could live? So your child could live? I didn't blame any of them, past the fact that they had made no preparations at all. The problem was, sooner or later they would run out of other people's stuff. Then, it was going to get ugly, especially for places like the farm. Everybody knows there's food on farms; that's where it comes from, after all. We were going to have to plan for that, as soon as we got out there. Security was going to be priority one.

"I don't know how helpful they might be, but if we run into the Scanlins on the way to the farm, I'd like to offer to take them with us. I know they want to try to find their friends' farm, but we can still offer, especially since they have no way of knowing if their friends are there. Sean was smart enough to be carrying the guns on him. He was smart enough to spy a car sitting in the parking lot that could, and did, provide supplies for his family. He was smart enough to figure out the gal who came back was going to try to take the rest of their stuff, with her bat-wielding buddy. I think they could be assets. Sean will be motivated to find a place he considers safe for his family. Kate can shoot. When we get to the farm, to keep everything and everyone safe, it's going to be a numbers game. My vote is if we catch up to them on the road, we make the proposal."

Russ looked around at the group. No arguments from me. Like I said, I could see myself in their position. Brian was nodding.

"I thought the same, Russ. They seemed to be doing the best they could, under the circumstances—at least, once we got them off the road."

Yeah, walking down the road, out in the open, was easier, especially with little kids; however, it also made you an easy target for the bad guys. I was glad they had stopped to help them.

"I vote for bringing them in. All I can think is where we'd be if we didn't have the preps we do. Those guys who keep coming back are just the beginning of what the dregs of society will be throwing at us. How will they protect those little ones? I vote yes."

I had almost worked myself into a crying jag. Good grief, what was going on? Oh, wait—it was almost time for my monthly visitor. Great—just what I needed. Yes, I had prepped for that too.

Bob and Janet made it unanimous. Russ was a good judge of character—look at Brian. We had all misjudged him. Russ saw something the rest of us didn't, when he saw him in a different situation. I trusted his judgement implicitly.

"Okay, now that that's settled, we need to get ready to pull out first thing in the morning. It's not bad out there yet, and given the loss of the houses up by the mall, I think we'd be better off leaving sooner than we planned. Those people will get here at some point. It's the natural path from where they are toward town, which is the natural instinct for the uninformed. They think more people, more chance for help. The reality is what we know—more people, less resources, more danger. There are also still people out there who think getting to a city or town is where the 'government' will assist them in this crisis. Brian and I have been out twice, and we haven't seen any sign of government, or law enforcement, or anything resembling authority. Another reason to go ahead and get out, before something like that shows up and starts ordering people around, or worse, confiscating resources for the 'greater good.'"

Russ looked at me. "What's left to go in the trailers?"

I thought for a second. "Whatever food we have left in the kitchen, and whatever you guys need to get loaded. The clothes we kept out. We emptied the Faraday cabinets of everything but the generators, and any big power tools you guys had, and got all that in. The rest of the guns and ammo—we didn't load any of that. The chickens and rabbits, obviously. We'll also have the bed of our truck and the back of Bob's SUV."

When I said it out loud, it was impressive how much we had gotten loaded. It was probably 90 to 95 percent of the stuff. Apparently, from the smile on his face, Russ agreed.

"That's awesome, babe! That'll save us a boatload of time! What do you think, Bob? An hour, two tops?"

"If that. With Brian and the boys for muscle, we can finish in no time. Great job, ladies!"

Janet and I fist bumped and grinned at everybody. Yeah, we rock.

"Okay, then let's get going with—" A knock on the door stopped Russ. "Who the hell could that be? If it's the Baxters, I'm kicking somebody's ass."

He pulled his pistol out and went to the door. Brian and Bob automatically followed with their guns drawn. Russ looked out the peephole. He pulled back, with a completely baffled look on his face. We waited for him to tell us who it was, but he holstered his pistol, reached for the door knob, and opened the door.

On the porch was a woman who looked like she had been through every ditch and sticker bush in the state. Her hair looked like a bird had nested in it, her clothes were torn and filthy, and she had more cuts on her than I felt one person could have and not be bleeding out. She raised her head and looked in. Russ looked her in the eye and said one word.

"Marietta?"

\*\*\*\*

Marietta Sampson was the epitome of a "rich bitch," in my opinion. She always had her makeup and nails done, never a hair out of place, even first thing in the morning. It was like she rolled out of bed looking like that. It wasn't natural.

As I said in the beginning, I thought she had designs on my husband. She was one of those "touchy" women. When she talked to him, she would put her hand on his arm, give it a little squeeze. I wasn't jealous, or threatened. My husband loves me, and I truly think he had no idea she was making passes at him. Actually, I kind of felt sorry for her. Widowed at thirty would suck. She seemed to be one of those women who needed a strong man in her life. Sorry, Marietta, but you can't have mine. Move along, sister. But Russ had a soft spot for seemingly helpless women, so when she called, he went. I think he felt sorry for her too.

185

Standing on our porch was a different woman. This woman looked like she had been through hell. Initially she seemed to have nothing but the clothes on her back, but she turned slightly and I saw a backpack of sorts. Actually, it seemed to be a purse with strings instead of straps, and it looked like it was hanging on by only one or two of those. But then, I wouldn't have expected Marietta to have a BOB. Her clothes were almost unrecognizable, but looked like they might be jeans, a T-shirt, and a hoodie. Shoes that had once been top-of-the-line sneakers were caked with mud, no longer a fashion statement. There was not one trace of makeup, and her hair, the bird's nest, looked to be pinned up in some fashion. This was a woman who had been on the road, for a while.

"Oh my God, Russ, I can't believe I found you! I can't believe you're here! Everything went off, and I couldn't call you to help me get it back on; and then I found out everybody's went off, and no one came to help, not the power company, or the police, nobody. And people started breaking into houses on my street, and I was scared because I was alone, and I didn't know what to do, but I knew I couldn't stay by myself, so I got your card and a city map, and I figured out how to get here, because I knew you'd know what to do. I got some cheese and crackers, some dried meat, and some bottles of water and put them in this bag. I started walking a few days ago, and there were men out there, grabbing women and dragging them off to the woods, and I got scared again, and I ran to the woods, in the other direction, and I hid until the bad men got finished and left."

I don't think she took a breath through that whole thing—but she wasn't finished. "I was afraid to leave the woods, but I didn't know how to get here if I didn't use the street, but I remembered the sun rises in the east, and on the map it was east to get to your house, so I stayed in the woods as long as I could, and ran when I had to get on the street. I had to run from bad men a couple of times, but I didn't stop, because I needed to get here, to be safe. I slept in the woods, under leaves to keep warm, and there were bugs and mosquitos and it was awful. But I knew I had to get here, because you'd help me. I made it, so can you help me, Russ? I really don't have anyone else to turn to, and I have nowhere else to go."

Bless her heart. That must have been hell. Then, as if we couldn't be any more shocked, Brian spoke up. "Marietta—Ms. Sampson? Is that you?" Now we all looked at Brian. How did he know her?

"Brian? Brian Riggins? What are you doing here?"

So, they did know each other.

"Ms. Sampson—Marietta—is a client. I've helped her with some estate planning."

Marietta was nodding, and looking at Russ again. "Russ, can I come in? I feel very exposed out here."

Russ visibly gained control of his wits again. He hesitated, but then opened the door wider. "Yes, come in, Marietta. Just don't plan on staying."

# Chapter 17

Marietta walked in, looking shocked. I don't think she'd expected Russ to respond that way. Of course, she didn't understand that everything had changed since she last saw him. Well, she knew everything had changed, she just didn't know how much *he* had. She stopped just inside the door, as Russ closed it behind her. She looked at Brian again, then back to Russ.

"I know I wasn't invited, but Russ, I can't go back out there, not alone. Do you know what it's like out there? There are no police. Assholes are just doing whatever they want to whoever they want. The stores are all empty, there's no food. I have nowhere to go. I can pay you—I have cash."

Seems she understood a little bit of it. Russ looked at her and shook his head. "What can I do with cash? Where can I spend it? You said yourself, the stores are empty. If cash will still buy you something, it won't for long. I have to think of my family first, Marietta. I can't take from them to give to someone else."

From her perspective, he must have sounded like an asshole, but from mine, he was a hero. Nothing came before his family.

She started crying. "Then tell me where I should go, what I should do! I don't know what's going on! I don't know what happened! I'm all alone! Please, help me!"

She half cried, half yelled. Brian stepped up. "Russ, can I talk to you a second? In private?"

Russ nodded, and the two headed out to the sunroom. The rest of us stood there, kind of awkward like.

I went over to Marietta. "Can I get you something to eat? Drink? Would you like to clean up a bit?" She looked at me with eyes full of tears, but assented.

"Yes, please—Anne, right? Russ talks about you and Rusty all the time. I haven't eaten since yesterday. The food I brought ran out. I was metering the water, and it ran out a couple of hours ago. So, yes, food and water would be about the best things that could happen to me at this moment."

I led her to the kitchen and fixed her some leftovers. I offered to heat it, but she declined. "I'm so hungry, I could eat a horse, so cold is fine." She all but inhaled the food, and acted like the glass of tea was the finest vintage wine ever. "Oh, Anne, thank you so much. I had no idea cold pasta and iced tea could taste so good. Did you say something about being able to clean up?"

I smiled at her, nodded, and led her to the basin in the down-stairs bathroom. I told her if she needed to use the toilet, just let me know and I would show her how to use the bucket of water on the floor to flush it. Believe it or not, not everyone knows how a toilet works. Another one of those things we take for granted.

She looked so grateful, I almost cried for her. "Thank you again for your kindness. I won't be a minute."

****

Brian and Russ went out to the sunroom and closed the door. Russ had a feeling he knew what Brian was going to say, that he was going to ask that Marietta be allowed to stay. Not that he was totally against it. Marietta was one of the best customers he had, if not the best. In her own way, she had paid for some of the preps we had. He also had a newfound respect for the woman. Walking here, alone, with the clothes on her back, and some peanut butter crackers and a couple of bottles of water? Not that he knew she had carried peanut butter crackers, but he doubted she'd had much food at her house that was bug out worthy. She was definitely one of the last people he expected to see standing on the porch.

"So, what's on your mind, Brian?" Russ sat on the edge of the table.

Brian started slowly. "Russ, I know you have rules about who comes into the group, and I'm very thankful you included me. I didn't have nearly as many supplies as you all have, and I will be working to repay your kindness for years—maybe the rest of my life, since I'll likely have one now. And I know Marietta, Ms. Sampson, isn't bringing anything to the table, but I'd like for the group to consider bringing her in. She and I met at my office. I helped her set up some long-term investments with some of her inheritance, not that that's going to do her any good now. We went out for coffee a couple of weeks ago. Turns out, she and I have a *lot* in common. She grew up with nothing, like me. I was going to call her this week, to see if she'd like to go to dinner. The thing is, if we'd had the time, she and I could very easily have been dating in the not-too-distant future. So, my question is, if she had been at my house, when this all went down, would you have included her in the invitation to join your family?"

Russ considered what Brian had told him and what he was asking. "Well, Brian, there's no knowing how differently this would have turned out had Marietta been at your house. Would you have been as open to what I told you in that situation, about what was happening? Maybe you would have approached us to take you both in, had you had her wellbeing to think about, too. Maybe you never would have come over that first day, so as not to appear weak, or less knowledgeable in front of her. I'm surprised you haven't brought her up since this went down, wanting to go check on her, something."

Brian looked down, face full of remorse. "I didn't know her address. Everything was on my phone or computer. I didn't think there was any way to find out. What were the chances you knew her, even better than me? And honestly, I have no idea how different the situation would have been had she been in the picture already. I hope I would have been smart enough to ask somebody what the hell was going on. I'm just really glad it was you."

Russ smiled at that. "You know the decision is not totally mine. I need to talk to everyone, without Marietta there. Another mouth to feed and another life to protect is what it boils down to. We need to have a meeting."

Brian looked hopeful. "Thank you, Russ. I want you to know that, if you choose to accept her, I will do whatever I can to pay both our ways. If that's extra security duty, hunting for food, you name it, it's done."

Russ headed for the door. "I don't think that will be necessary. Let's get inside. If you'll bring Marietta out here and fill her in, the rest of us can talk in the house."

**\*\*\*\***

As Russ and Brian came into the kitchen, we all looked their way. Marietta had cleaned up as best she could in a basin and at least gotten a brush through her hair, which was now pulled up in a much neater ponytail. Brian smiled at her and spoke first.

"Marietta, can you come outside with me?" She nodded and followed him out to the sunroom.

Russ motioned to the living room. "We need to talk. Come sit with me, all of you."

We all filed into the living room. Russ shared Brian's story with us. I was empathetic to his plight. Janet seemed to feel the same. We're chicks—it's the whole new love thing. We're suckers for it.

Bob spoke up. "That would put us to eight. Not that we can't feed that many, easy. I thought she was a hoity-toity, can't break a nail gal. Is she going to be dead weight? Can she cook, clean, shoot?"

"I don't know, Bob, but Brian said he'll do whatever he needs to do to 'pay' her way. Brian has been completely loyal since the day he moved in. He hasn't asked for anything from us. He's stepped up, without being asked, every time we've needed him. I have no issue with giving him this one. Personally, I'm impressed as hell she got here. There's obviously more to her than we first thought."

We all agreed and voted unanimously to add another body to our household.

Bob offered another question. "Where's she gonna sleep? I don't think we should expect them to automatically shack up just because they had coffee together. He'd have to buy me dinner first, for damn sure." That cracked us up.

"Okay, Romeo, calm down," Russ said. "We still have the sofa in the living room, and it will only be for tonight. We are still heading out first thing in the morning. I think the time is now, before there are raiders and marauders on the road out of here. Let's get them in here."

Russ went to the door to the sunroom, opened it, and called them in. They both looked nervous, with Marietta bordering on panic. Again, I could commiserate with her. If I were in her position, I would be too. He brought them into the living room and motioned for them to sit. Once they were perched on the edge of the couch, he began.

"We talked it over, and if you'd like to stay with us, Marietta, you're welcome."

Brian broke out into a huge grin, and Marietta jumped up and squealed. Russ smiled, but motioned for her to calm down.

"I need to let you know the rest. We are heading out of here first thing in the morning. This place is not safe, and we're not staying to see how bad it gets. We have a place to go, and you can join us there. We'll probably be there for a long time. If that works for you, then we're good."

She was grinning, nodding, and trying not to bounce up and down like a little kid on Christmas morning. "Yes, yes, yes! I'd love to join you all, wherever you go. Brian told me how you brought him in, and I'm so grateful you are willing to let me in as well. I don't have a lot with me, but I do have a few of my late husband's guns in my other bag, with ammo. I would be more than happy to donate them to the community arsenal."

Bob asked the question I think we were all considering. "What other bag?"

We hadn't seen anything with her other than the flimsy purse she'd brought in. She grinned and went to the door. She went out and reached behind the boxwoods in front of the house, and pulled out a big duffel bag that looked pretty loaded down.

"I didn't know for sure if you would be here, so I didn't want to take the chance someone else was here and might take this. I got most of his guns and as much ammo as I felt like I could handle. The bag weighs a ton, but it has rollers on one end, so I rolled it a good bit of the way. I made sure to hide it when I saw or heard other people, but I had this on me the whole time." She lifted her jacket and shirt to reveal what appeared to be a Colt 1911. Damn, big gun for a little gal. Apparently I wasn't the only one who thought so.

"Can you shoot that? Have you shot it?" Brian looked skeptical.

Marietta kind of smirked at him. "Yes to both, and quite well. Tim, my husband, made sure I knew how to load and shoot every gun he owned. I can't tell you how many hours I spent at the range. The officers there said I was a natural. Oh, and I have my concealed carry permit, not that it matters anymore."

Marietta had turned out to be someone completely different than we had first assumed. While she wasn't much for DIY and maintenance, she had experience and a history that could both be valuable in the days, weeks, months, and possibly years to come. I think Russ had another recruit for security detail here. She opened the bag and pulled out pistols, revolvers, a Mossberg 500 tactical shotgun, a 30-30 rifle with a scope, along with ammo for all of them. Not a lot—she was right about the weight. But all the guns were fully loaded, and she had at least one full box of ammo for each caliber. The guys' eyes all lit up when she pulled out a case. Inside was a Desert Eagle 1911, stainless. Beautiful gun.

"I couldn't just throw this one in the bag. It had to stay protected. It was his favorite."

The sad smile told of the love she had lost when her husband died. I'd have to ask how that happened one day. Not today though; we had other things to do. Sadly, that was getting ready to leave our home.

**\*\*\*\***

We spent the rest of the afternoon doing just that. Russ pulled our truck out of the garage and into the backyard. He and Bob put the rotor button back on Bob's SUV. The trailers were hooked up to the vehicles and pulled out so we could get them open to put the rest of the stuff in. Rather than keeping them back against the fence, they set the rigs up so that all we had to do was load the animals and us in the morning and head out. They did pull the distributor caps back off both of them, removing the rotor buttons again—redneck anti-theft practices in a post-apocalyptic world.

We loaded everything that was left from the cabinets, as well as all the food we still had out. Tonight would be a buffet of anything we had left in the freezer. We kept two camp stoves out for heating multiple foods, and we held back instant oatmeal for breakfast, and coffee, of course. Everything else was loaded up. We decided to use disposable dishes, so we wouldn't have to worry about cleaning duty, and packed up the regular stuff to go. The trailers were stacked and packed as full as we could get them. There was no wasted space, and very little left over.

We didn't have room inside for the bikes and Brian's trailer, but the bikes were strapped to the top of the big trailers, and the bike trailer was actually collapsible; they broke it down and put it in the back of the truck.

We had roof cargo haulers for both vehicles, and those were filled with clothes, shoes, linens, everything we had been using in the house. The sheets and blankets on the beds now would be stripped as soon as we got up in the morning and added to the top of the pile. Yes, we had these things out at the farm, but it's not like there were going to be factories making new ones any time soon. Same with the clothes and shoes—we were bringing a lot, but we had no way of knowing when, or if, we'd be able to get replacements. We had to plan for if not.

With everything pretty much loaded, we decided to get cleaned up as best we could. We didn't know if we'd have trouble getting to the farm the next day, so it could be a while before we would be in a position to bathe again. We brought in the four sun showers. Four bags, with four gallons in each one for eight people—that was going to be tight. Get wet, lather everything up, rinse off, and make it quick. Janet and I decided to heat water from one of the waterBOBs and do it the old-fashioned way. We also made an offer to Marietta to join our "girls' night."

"I'd love to. What do we need to do?"

We grabbed one of the camp stoves, a big stock pot, and one of the canning pots I had left out for this purpose. I handed the stock pot to Marietta, the canner to Janet, and took the camp stove myself.

"Ladies, follow me. Gentlemen, we'll need about an hour. You are in charge of your own cleansing, and monitor the boys. You can use all the sun showers. Go out back and do it community style. Keep your drawers on though, in case anyone is snooping around out there. You don't want to get caught with your pants down—or off, as the case may be." They laughed, grabbed the showers and towels, and headed out back.

We gals went upstairs to the master bath. We had used the water in this tub's waterBOB first, so it was already empty. We had folded it up and put it in one of the trailers. We set the stove up on the bathroom counter and put the stock pot on it full of water to boil. We took the canning pot, filled it about halfway with cold water, and set it by the tub. As we worked, we explained to Marietta what we were going to do.

"Since you've gone the longest without, if you want to go first, you are welcome to, Marietta. Basically, we strip down and get in the tub. With things the way they are, I'd say keep your under-things on, so they can get a washing too. We'll mix hot water from the stove with the cold water in the canner, keep it as warm as we can, and pour it over your head, getting your whole body wet. Then, you lather up, starting with your hair, and work your way down. When you're done, we'll pour the water over your head again. We'll try to keep it warm, but depending on how long it takes you to get lathered up, it might be tepid by the time you're ready to rinse. We'll have more water heating if we need it for yours, and if not, it will be used on the next one. This way we can be a little more liberal with the water if we need to, since it usually takes us a bit more to get our hair rinsed and such. Sound good?"

Marietta nodded, but seemed a bit apprehensive.

Janet said, "Honey, if you're shy, you'll need to get over that real quick. We are all about to be as close as humanly possible. When we get to the farm, there is one house, six bedrooms, and two and a half bathrooms. All the bedrooms will be full, so you and Brian will probably end up in the attic or the basement. We'll figure that out when we get there. What I'm trying to say is there will be ten of us in the house, and we will soon know everything there is to know about each other. Are you okay with that?"

Marietta gave her a slight smile. "I'm sorry, I'm not trying to be difficult. I've never really had any women friends. When you're considered rich, people are either jealous of you or intimidated by you. I don't know how to act with women, you know, just us girls. I'm excited, but scared, you know?"

Janet and I both looked at her and smiled back. "We've been friends for over ten years now. We know each other like sisters. We will do our best to help you join 'the family.'" I did the air quotes and everything.

She laughed, and started stripping off her nasty clothes. "Okay, sisters, let's get clean."

<br>

\*\*\*\*

<br>

Janet and Marietta were close to the same size, so Janet brought her some clean clothes. I thought Marietta was going to cry. You'd have thought we'd taken her on a shopping spree or something. Marietta got dressed, and Janet went next. We kept water heating, even after I got my "shower." We plugged the tub and threw Marietta's traveling outfit in. We poured the rest of the hot water in, then about the same amount of cold, and dumped in a bit of body wash. Soap is soap, as far as I'm concerned. We took the plunger from the linen closet and created some action in the water. We did a little scrubbing, and the water turned dark. We drained the tub, plugged it back up, and dumped cold water in. We swooshed it around to get the soap out, then wrung the clothes out as tight as we could. We pulled the plug again, then hung the clothes over the shower curtain rod.

I turned to Marietta. "I doubt they'll be dry by morning, but they'll be in a lot better shape than they were when you got here. We'll hang them out when we get to the farm."

Marietta looked on the verge of tears. "Thank you so much, Anne. I don't know what I would have done if you all hadn't still been here. If it had taken me one more day to get here, you wouldn't have been. I can't even bear to think of what I would have had to do."

I hesitated just a moment, then wrapped my arms around her, giving her one of my famous snug hugs. "Well, you won't be finding that out. You are part of our family. Now that we smell better, let's go get some food in everyone's bellies."

We went to the kitchen and pulled everything out of the freezer. We had spaghetti, shit on a shingle, some soup, a few pork chops, hot dogs—no buns though—and a few helpings of a number of different veggies. Not enough of one thing to feed everybody, but more than enough of a lot of little things to fill us up.

The boys wanted hot dogs. There were a few slices of loaf bread left, so they made do with that in place of buns. The compromise was they had to eat a veggie with it; they chose green beans. We set them up at the breakfast bar, so we'd have room for all the adults at the table. We warmed up what needed to be heated over a couple of the camp stoves. We set up a buffet type line, and everyone filled their plates. We had tea and water to drink. We sat at the dining room table and started to plan out our trip to the farm.

"I'll take the lead, Bob will follow," Russ said. "Since he has a back seat, Brian and Marietta will have to ride with them. I'll take the animals in the truck. We'll cover the bed with a tarp, so no one can see what's in there at a glance. We need to cover what's in the back of the SUV with a tarp as well. The less people can see, the better the chance we don't get stopped. I don't know what we are going to come up on out there, so we need to be vigilant and ready for anything. We're going to stand watch tonight in the sunroom, so we can keep an eye on the rigs. We should be able to hear anything that happens outside from out there, the way sound travels now.

"I want everyone who is not on watch in bed sleeping tonight, including watch buddies. If anything happens, we can come get help. I don't expect the scavengers back, at least not tonight. I'm pretty sure our show of force will have them moved on, for now. By the time they get back down our street, we'll be long gone. The Baxters should have raided enough from the empty houses to hold them for a while, so I expect them to still be asleep when we head out. I want us to be on the road as soon as possible, but I don't want us to forget anything. We'll get up, eat breakfast, and go through the house one more time. I want to put the boards up on the windows before we leave. I don't doubt that someone will break in here sooner or later, but I don't want it to be easy for them.

"We'll let the ladies gather the linens, any clothes left, and any food we can take. Rusty and Ben can pen up the animals. Brian, Bob, and I will take care of the windows and get the vehicles ready to go. Can anybody think of anything else we need to do before we leave tomorrow?"

We all looked at each other, but no one offered any other input. So, this was it. We were leaving first thing in the morning. We were leaving our home, possibly for good. I was close to tears. My heart was hurting. We had lived in that house for most of Rusty's life. I had my chicken pen, rabbit hutch, and garden out back. Russ planted the trees in the front yard the year we moved in. There was so much of our lives rooted here, and I wasn't ready to let it go. The next day was going to suck so bad. But, if the choice was stay, where we were close to too many desperate people who could potentially hurt us, or worse, or get to the farm, where there weren't a lot of people close, and we had almost unlimited resources for food and water—there was no choice. We had to go. I hoped I would sleep that night.

# Chapter 18

Russ woke me up early, just before dawn. "Anne, we need to get moving."

I stretched, grumbled, and got up. The smell of coffee pulled me into the kitchen. Janet was already up, dressed, with a coffee cup held out to me. Bless this woman. The tea kettle started whistling, so she pulled it off the stove. She had eight paper bowls set out with instant oatmeal. The boys came down the stairs, followed by Bob, and stumbled to the table. Janet mixed their oatmeal and took it to the table.

Ben looked at his mother. "Mom, it's too early. I can't eat yet."

Janet set the bowl in front of him. "Sorry, honey, but you're going to need to wake up, and quick. You and Rusty have animals to get penned up, then see if your dads need any help with final preps. We need to be out of here as soon as possible."

Ben's head dropped back down to his chest, and he fake snored. That got everyone tickled. He raised his head, smiled, and grabbed his spoon. I must admit, I was with him. I'm not a big breakfast person. Yes, I know, the most important meal of the day, gets your metabolism started, yada yada yada. I just prefer to eat like an hour or so after I get up. But, I'd try to set a good example; I picked up a bowl myself.

We ate and cleaned up the kitchen. We had thermoses we filled with more coffee. I was pretty sure we'd need it. After tooth brushing, everyone headed off to their appointed duties. Marietta joined Janet and me upstairs, where we started stripping beds. The sheets weren't clean, but they weren't disgusting either, so we folded them, somewhat, to make them easier to handle. We put sheets and any extra pillow cases into one pillow case per set. That would keep them together. We could wash them when we got to the farm. We stuffed the pillows into more trash bags.

We gathered up any clothes we could find. Most of our clothing was already loaded in the trailers; we had kept out just enough to get us through a couple of weeks, including washing. We hadn't done all the laundry, due to the time frame being moved up on us, so we tossed anything dirty into trash bags. Clean got loaded into suitcases and duffel bags. With no way of knowing how long things would be down, we couldn't afford to leave anything of use behind. Shoes went into another trash bag. We didn't worry about whose were whose—in the coming months, we would be wearing whatever fit, especially Marietta, who hadn't been able to bring any with her.

We went through every room, every closet, every cabinet and drawer. We grabbed anything we thought we might need, which was pretty much everything. All we left was furniture. We didn't have room for the beds and chests, plus we had that already set up out at the farm. We took everything down to the bottom of the stairs. Ben and Rusty were coming in from the garage, carrying chicken cages.

"When you guys get finished loading the animals, you can take these bags out to the trailers. Nothing breakable, so they can be stuffed anywhere there's a spot. Let your dads know."

I pointed to the trash bags and the duffels. We had a few breakables from the bathrooms, but those were in a box we'd kept separate. They nodded and continued out to the sunroom. We moved on to the kitchen.

We had packed up everything possible the day before, so we just had a few utensils and two of the camp stoves. We washed what we had used after breakfast and packed it all up. The paper plates from the night before and bowls from breakfast went into trash bags. We'd take them out to the farm and burn them at night, when the smoke wouldn't be easily seen. We kept out travel mugs for everyone, and a case of bottled water for each vehicle. Everything else got sent to the backyard with the boys. We kept out protein bars, peanut butter, crackers, canned sausages, jerky, the last of the radishes that were ready from the garden, as well as the last of the lettuce. We also had MREs, which I hoped we wouldn't have to eat. Not my favorites. We put some freeze-dried meals, which only needed boiling water added to them, in the trucks, just in case we didn't make it to the farm that day. That thirty-minute drive would probably be a lot longer, and if something happened to hold us up, it could take more than a day. We wanted to be ready for anything.

It took a couple of hours to get the last of it loaded. By then the sun was up, but it was still early, not eight yet. Russ and Bob had gone over to Bob and Janet's to see if there was anything of use still there, and Brian and Marietta had gone to Brian's for the same final look. They all came back with clothes, missed in the attics from seasonal storage. Again, we couldn't afford to leave anything, since we had no way of knowing if, or when, manufacturing plants would be able to start back up. We crammed everything we could in the trailers, stuffing every available space with clothes. We could sort it all out when we got to the farm.

Last walk-throughs done, Janet and I must have had the same thought at the same time—we were leaving our homes, possibly for good. We both got weepy and hugged each other while the tears flowed. At least we all had each other. Had this happened during the day, while Bob and I were at work and the boys at school, how much different would this scenario have played out? Would we all have been able to get home? Would we have been able to get to the boys? In my mind, those answers were yes. Both of us had EMP-resistant vehicles, and I had no doubt Russ would have gotten to Rusty and me come hell or high water. But there was also no way of knowing what obstacles could have presented themselves to hinder his efforts. We already knew there were abandoned cars and trucks everywhere. Had Russ been required to retrieve us, he would have had to broadcast to everyone out there stranded that first day that we had a vehicle that still worked.

I could just imagine the turmoil that the world had been in those first couple of days. Most people would have had no idea what was happening. They would have expected anyone with a running vehicle to be "neighborly" and give them a ride home, or on to work—those that didn't get that work, as in jobs that paid money, was not what they were going to be doing now. When Russ had passed them by, as he surely would have, they might have yelled, flipped him off, whatever rude gesture or thought came to mind. There might possibly have been a mob mentality already, where they would have tried to band together to get him to stop and help, trying to bar his way. It could have been bad, really bad. If we had anything to be thankful for in this life-changing event, it was the timing of the pulse. We talked about that, wiped our tears, and started for the sunroom. It was time to leave.

****

Russ, Bob, and Brian spent the next thirty minutes putting plywood over the windows in both houses. While nothing we had done would keep anyone out that really wanted in, the thought was that if we made it difficult enough they might give up and move on.

Not really likely, as desperate people will do whatever they have to in order to survive. The only thing we could do was try to protect our homes, in case we were able to come back some day. Brian didn't have the supplies to do the same at his house, but he had a great attitude about it.

"It's a roof and four walls full of 'things.' The past week, I have found out exactly what is important in life. Food and water, shelter, and friends who have your back. The other stuff is just that—stuff. If someone wants to break in to see if I left anything, hopefully it will be someone who needs it, not that there's anything of value left over there."

He was right, and it made the guys feel kind of bad for shutting the place up like they had, in case someone out there really needed a place to go, but it was done. Besides, it wasn't our responsibility to take care of them, not anymore. We had to take care of us first.

We had the trucks loaded to the max, along with the trailers. We had left room for our bodies, our travel food and water, and that was about it. Every other spare spot was filled, as well as the rooftop cargo carriers on each vehicle. Russ and Bob went out front, into the street, to see who might be out and about. They didn't see or hear anyone, so we decided it was time. They came back in and bolted the front door. Russ unlocked the gate from the backyard and opened it wide. We loaded everyone into the vehicles, and Russ closed and locked the back door before getting in our truck. He started it, and that signaled Bob to start his as well; with both vehicles running, there was nothing else to do but head out. I tried, but I couldn't stop the tears from flowing again. I loved our home. I couldn't believe we were leaving it, but I knew we couldn't stay. Russ reached over and squeezed my hand, then keyed the mike on the two-way radio. "Bob, can you hear me okay?"

Bob replied immediately. "Five by five, buddy. Let's get to the farm."

We pulled both rigs out and stopped so Bob could go back and lock the gate up. Again, if someone wanted in bad enough, they could get in, but we had to do what we could to try to dissuade them. Russ watched in his side view mirror as Bob reached through the two sides of the gate and latched and locked the hasp. He ran back to his SUV, gave us a thumbs up, and jumped in. Russ pulled out onto the street and headed toward the interstate, with Bob right behind us. We were on our way to a new home, with new friends. I had my fingers crossed we would make it safe, and soon.

# Chapter 19

We no sooner got off our street, maybe a mile down the road, than we saw signs of recent activity in the area. Apparently, the inhabitants of the burned-out neighborhood by the mall were making their way to our neighborhood, just like Russ had predicted. There were people walking, pushing shopping carts full of whatever meager belongings they had been able to either salvage from their homes or scavenge from others, from the looks of it. There were families, couples, and individuals, all seemingly migrating together to … Did they even know where they were going? What they might be walking into? Did they care? If you had nothing, or almost nothing, anything was an improvement. They were dirty and seemed to be rather thin, or they were wearing clothes that had not originally belonged to them. How long had it been now? Over a week, maybe a week and a half. Would people starve that fast? No, but going from three meals a day to one or none would definitely make a difference. These were the kind of people we were hoping to avoid. These were the ones who would be getting desperate, who would do whatever they had to do to feed their families. These were the dangerous ones—the ones who had nothing to lose.

Russ grabbed the two-way. "Bob, no matter what happens, don't stop, don't slow down. In fact, if anyone steps out in front of you, gun it. They'll move or die. If they move, we keep going and say a prayer for them. If they don't and we have to kill one of them, the rest will back off. Everybody get your guns out, and make sure they're visible to them. Brian, open your window and stick a rifle barrel out, so they can see it. This is the new world, gang, and it sucks. It sucks to be them, the ones who didn't prepare for the unknown, and it sucks to be us, who did, and now we have to watch others suffer and die. No hesitation, buddy. Stay on my ass."

Bob radioed back. "I hear ya. I got ya. I'm right behind ya."

Russ kept going, heading for the interstate. The people on the side of the road looked up, staring at us. Their eyes seemed to light up when they saw our vehicles, like we were saviors or something, but when they saw we weren't stopping, not even slowing down, their eyes changed. They seemed to take on a defiant look, like we were in some way treating them as inferior. Maybe we were. My heart went out to them. How awful to have to fight for your survival, for the lives of your family. But when it came down to it, my family was more important, to me at least. I pulled my pistol out of my holster and held it up at window level. The looks from the pedestrians didn't get any less vindictive, but they did back up from the road.

One guy seemed to be angling toward us, with a very menacing look. He was pointing at our truck, waving a bat, and yelling. "Hey! Stop! We need help! You can't just leave us here!"

Russ pushed the gas pedal harder, speeding up. Bob stayed right behind us. The yeller jumped out of the way just before Russ would have hit him. I looked in the side view mirror. He was running behind us, still yelling, though we couldn't hear what he said anymore. I looked over at Russ, but he shook his head and kept going.

The people on the sides of the road kept coming toward us, toward our street, I guess. I couldn't get over how many there were. It looked like more than could have been living in the burned-out area. That meant people were migrating from the cities now. Was it that bad, already? If the larger cities were working their way out to areas like ours, that meant the seventy-two-hour theory was right. It had been three times three days since the EMP. Supplies were gone in the larger metropolitan areas. People were out of food already. What would it be like in another two weeks? We couldn't get to the farm fast enough for me. We could only hope the migrants wouldn't go that far out, at least not for a while. Unfortunately for them, there was a really good chance some of them wouldn't live that long. Unfortunately for us, the ones who did last that long would probably not be the kind of folks we wanted to deal with. Hopefully, by then we would have our perimeter secure and the bodies to hold it. I was pretty sure we'd need every available person.

Just when it looked like we were going to get past the majority of the migrants, I saw a dirty woman coming up to the side of the road, pushing a stroller. Her clothes were almost rags, her face and hair were filthy; she was just pitiful to look at. She had a look of complete despair on her face, and it tore at my motherly instincts. She pushed through the crowd, and just as we were coming up to where she stood, she shoved the stroller in front of our truck. I screamed, and Russ swerved. He hit the stroller with the right front bumper of the truck, but kept going. In the side view mirror I saw the stroller flip up in the air and fall back to the street. The baby that had been in it flew into the air as well and landed on the street beside the woman. She looked down at the baby, then up at me in the mirror, with a very different expression. This one was pure hatred.

I grabbed Russ's arm. "Russ! We have to stop! We just killed that woman's child! We have to stop!"

Russ was shaking his head. He had a death grip on the steering wheel, and his whole body was shaking.

Brian came over the radio. "Keep going, Russ. It was a trick. We swerved to stay behind you, so I got a good look at the whole thing. It was a doll. She was trying to get you to stop, probably part of a gang that was looking to take our stuff. There was no baby. Do you copy?"

Russ slowly closed and opened his eyes, and with a still severely shaking hand, grabbed the radio. "I copy. Thank you, Brian. Let's get out of here."

I was still crying, my emotions completely unraveled. I was mad at the woman for trying to make us think we had done something so horrendous. I was upset that, had it been a real child, we still would have had to keep going, because we couldn't take the chance that what she had tried to make happen actually did. I was scared of what this world was already becoming, that people could think of something so despicable, to try to trick someone so they could steal from them, maybe even kill them for their meager belongings. I was shocked that Russ was able to keep going, even before he'd known it was a ruse, though I could tell how badly it had shaken him up.

Mostly, I was sad—to think that mankind could sink so low, so fast. From the scavengers that had been on our street within a couple of days, breaking into homes and taking whatever they wanted, to our neighbors, thinking someone else would take care of them—or should, in their minds—and expecting those who had something, who had planned for a disaster, to share with them just because they didn't plan past tomorrow; to the woman just now, who would play on the basest of human instincts—to protect our children, all children, from harm—to get us to stop so she, and probably her group, could try to overwhelm us and take everything we had worked so hard to gather, preparing for a situation like the one we found ourselves in. Because they hadn't prepared, they had chosen the path of marauder, a viable path if you had the manpower and the weapons. The fact that she had tried to get us to stop meant they probably had both.

I had no sooner had the thought about the weapons someone in that crowd might have than a shot rang out. Russ still had the radio in his hand.

"Guys? What's happening? Where'd that shot come from?"

Brian immediately came back. "Some guy stepped out of the crowd into the street behind us and shot at us. I think he hit the trailer, but we're not stopping to find out. Keep going! Haul ass!"

Russ pressed the gas pedal harder. We heard more shots, but they sounded farther away. He handed me the radio. "Check on them. I need to keep both hands on the wheel, going this fast, hauling the trailer."

I keyed the radio. "Brian? Are you guys still okay? We heard more shots."

"Yeah, Anne, we're fine. I don't know where those came from, but they were further back than the first one. Probably more from that group, *voicing* their frustration at not getting us to stop."

His emphasis on "voicing" got us to smile a bit. I glanced at Rusty; he looked pretty shook up. I wrapped my arms around him.

"It's okay, honey. We're okay. It wasn't what it looked like. Are you alright?"

He nodded slowly and laid his head on my shoulder. I smoothed his messy hair off his forehead and planted a kiss on it. Damn them for that, too, for scaring *my* baby.

We got to the ramp for the interstate. Russ slowed down and looked around. He reached for the radio. I handed it to him and took to looking around myself.

"What are we looking for, baby?"

"Anything or anybody. Once we get on the interstate and get a few miles down the road, if we can we'll pull over for a few minutes so everyone can take a quick break. I think we could use one after that mess."

I nodded. "I could definitely do with a bathroom break. It may be too late—I think I pissed myself back there."

He gave me a little smile. "That makes two of us."

He keyed the radio. "Guys, we're going to take it slow up the ramp. I want to make sure there is no one around who might try to stop us. Keep your eyes peeled and shout out if you see or hear anything. Roll the windows down a bit so you can hear what's going on outside. Once we get a few miles between us and that group back there, we'll pull over for a quick break. Sound good?"

Bob had the radio back. "Sounds great. Let's get this done!"

Russ handed the radio back to me. "If you see or hear any-thing, let me know, then let them know. Ready?"

I gave him a quick nod in the affirmative, and he picked up speed a bit, but still went slow enough that we could get a good look at the surrounding area. I didn't see anything, outside of a lot of abandoned cars. No people at all. No sound—that was the weirdest part. No engines, no horns, no exhaust, nothing. It was freaking me out a little. How long before those sounds were a part of our lives again? Would they ever be?

Russ was getting to the top of the ramp. So far, so good.

"Tell them we're going to pick up speed now, Anne. We're not going to go seventy, but we are going to try to get some miles behind us, then find a safe place to stop for a few minutes."

I relayed the information back to the others, and Brian replied, "Sounds good, looks clear. Let us know if you see anything. We'll do the same."

We picked up speed, to about forty, forty-five miles per hour. Fast enough to get somewhere, but slow enough to be able to scope out the area and stop without killing everyone if we had to. There had definitely been a path cleared here, which was concerning. Whoever had gone to the trouble of moving the abandoned vehicles out of the way did it for a reason, like they meant to be coming through here again. It was about three miles to the next exit, then the road narrowed to two lanes in each direction. If we could get that far without trouble, we should be in a better area. It got very rural from there on out, so hopefully scavengers would think it was too much trouble, with the houses so far apart.

We tried to check every spot on the sides of the roads, especially any that looked like they might have been set up, like a hide. We did see some areas that looked suspicious, but there was no one in them. Russ had an opinion on that.

"My guess is they were used early on, when people were trying to make their way home, or anywhere, in the first few days. They would have been walking with whatever they had been able to carry from their cars, and most would have had no way to defend themselves. They would have been easy targets—scared, alone, no idea what was going on, wearing clothes and shoes *not* meant for that kind of travel. Can you imagine how it was out here? Hundreds of people, with little to no food and water, fighting for each other's lunch they had been planning to take to work that day? I don't know who did this, but I'm so thankful they did it when they did. You and Rusty were home. Bob got home quick. I don't even want to think about what it would have been like for you had it happened ten, twenty, or thirty minutes later."

As if to emphasize his thought, we saw a body lying in the weeds at the side of the road. I couldn't tell at that speed if it was a man or a woman, because it was already black and bloated. I turned my head away and saw Rusty staring at it.

"Don't look at it, honey. Look at the road."

Russ saw what we were seeing and sped up a bit. The radio came to life.

"Holy shit, Russ, did you see that? It was a body, a frickin' body!" Bob couldn't hide the shock in his voice.

Russ replied, "Yeah, I saw it. I don't think that will be the last one we see either. Let's get past that next exit, and see if we can find a place to pull over for a few minutes. Keep your eyes peeled."

The cars were getting thinner the further out we went. We were heading away from town, and most people would have been heading in to work. We did see more bodies, probably people who lived out this way, trying to get home. I saw one that was unmistakably female, because her clothes had been ripped from her body. She had probably been raped, then apparently strangled with what appeared to be her blouse. She'd been tossed in the ditch on the side of the road, like just another bag of garbage. It was all I could do not to throw up. I heard Rusty gag, quickly grabbed a plastic bag, and held it up for him. He waved me off.

"I'm alright, Mom. I know I have to get used to seeing stuff like that."

My heart broke. Why did my fifteen-year-old have to get used to that? Because some assholes had apparently set off a nuke in the atmosphere, and the world as we knew it was gone, and the new one was full of a bunch more assholes who did whatever the hell they wanted to, now that everything had gone to hell. I didn't retch, but I couldn't hold back the tears. I hated this new "normal."

****

We got close to the next exit, and Russ slowed down again. He got back on the radio.

"Guys, I think if we can get past this one, we should be in a better area. This exit is the last of the burbs, so I doubt the bad guys will be working their way south. My guess is they are concentrating on the places where there are multiple homes, more choices, more stuff. I say if it looks clear, we get a mile or so past this exit, then look for that stopping spot. Cool?"

"That's a big ten-four, good buddy. I need to drain the lizard. Ow! Damn, sugar! That hurt!"

Russ and I both busted out laughing at that, because we could picture it happening—Janet smacking Bob for the crude remark. Could have been a head shot, arm, gut—it didn't matter, she would have gotten him good.

"Thank you for the laugh, Janet," Russ said. "Good shot, wherever you got him. Seriously, stay sharp, gang. Yell out if you see anything."

Russ proceeded, slow but steady, toward the exit. I was trying to look in every direction at once.

Brian came on the radio. "Russ! I see people down the ramp on the right side!"

Russ grabbed the radio. "How many? Do you see any weapons? What are they doing?"

To me, he said, "Anne, see if you can see anything on your side."

I looked over the edge of the overpass, which we were almost on. There were maybe half a dozen men, a couple of women, and four or five kids, toddler to young teen. They were all looking toward us, but no one was making any move to come our way or bring any weapons to bear. I relayed all that to Russ, and right after that Brian came on the radio and said almost the exact same thing.

"Okay, if they don't want any trouble, we sure as hell don't, so just keep an eye on them, and we'll keep going."

Brian spoke again. "Russ, I think I see Sean Scanlin down there. I'm almost positive it's him!"

Russ slowed to a stop. "If it's them, they didn't get very far. Let's find out for sure. We told them we'd watch for them and give them a ride out to their friends' place, or as close as we could get them. Let's pull over. Everybody stay alert though. We're outnumbered."

Bob pulled over behind our rig. Brian got out and waved down to the people. "Sean? It's Brian Riggins. We met a few days ago. Are you guys alright?"

One of the men looked up, and with a big grin on his face, started up the ramp.

"Brian! Russ! I was hoping we'd see you guys again! You coming down here, or do you want us to come up to you?"

Brian looked at Russ, who was already shaking his head. "No, we'll come down to you. Give us a minute."

Russ went to Bob and Janet. "Brian and I will go down, since we know them, and we'll take Anne, for the female aspect. The rest of you stay up here. Don't leave the vehicles. Janet, you take the rear; Bob, you take point, and put the boys on either side. Keep an eye out for anything suspicious, or out of place. It looks pretty safe, but don't take any chances."

Bob nodded and directed everyone to their posts. Marietta went to the rear with Janet. The rest of us started down the ramp, sidearms visible.

The men were alert, herding the women and children together and behind them. Good for them. Placing themselves between their loved ones and danger was a good sign, a sign that they were good people. Russ was in the lead, with me behind him and Brian bringing up the rear, all watching the group, but keeping an eye on the surrounding area as well. Russ held his hand out to Sean as he approached them.

"Sean, so good to see you again. I'm glad you and your family are well—well, as well as can be expected in this new reality." Sean shook hands with Russ, smiling. "How are you all doing? I see you've found some others to travel with." Russ inclined his head toward the new folks. "Very good move. Hi, I'm Russ Mathews. This is my wife, Anne, and our friend, Brian."

The other men came forward and shook our hands. The women and children stayed back, but seemed to relax a bit.

Sean took over, making his own introductions. "Russ, Brian, this is Ryan, and his brother, Bill; Pete, Mike, and Lee. They lived in this area, about a mile from here. Sara is Pete's wife. They have one son, Tony. Lee has two kids, Moira and Aiden. His wife, Jackie, never made it home from work."

Russ shook hands all around, and paused at Lee. "I am so sorry for your loss. I don't know what I would have done if Anne hadn't still been at home when it happened."

Lee acknowledged the sentiment with tear-filled eyes. "Thank you. I still can't believe she didn't come home. We waited for four days, but there was no sign of her. We ran out of food and had to leave the house. I still have hope, but I know it's probably fruitless."

A single tear ran down his cheek. He wiped it away; I wiped at a few as well. I couldn't imagine going through this without Russ, and I knew he felt the same. Aiden was older, probably ten, and Moira looked to be about six or seven. They were as clean as could be expected in this situation. I was impressed. All of them looked tired, but not hungry, and semi clean. Apparently they had been doing alright so far.

"Hi, kids. I'm Anne. How are you guys doing? Have you eaten today?" I looked expectantly at Sara.

She smiled and shook her head. "Not yet. We were just about to try to find some greens or something in the woods there. We had a rabbit stew last night, so no one is starving."

I nodded and took her hand. "How about we all have something to eat? We have some supplies in the trucks, and it looks like it's probably about lunchtime. What do you think, Russ?"

He gave us a tight smile. "I think that would be a great idea. I have a huge hankering for some peanut butter and crackers. How about you guys?" He looked at the kids, who all had eyes as big as saucers.

It was Tony who spoke up first. "You have peanut butter, mister?" If you were a kid and had been eating off the land for a week or so, peanut butter would probably be the stuff dreams were made of. I must admit, there were times I craved it, and nothing but a big tablespoon of it would suffice. It was also high protein and high calorie, something these folks would need.

Russ leaned down to Tony's level. "We do, and if you guys will go over there and take a seat in the shade, we'll bring some to you."

I looked at Sara, and she smiled and nodded. I headed up the ramp.

While I went to get the food, Russ got the story on the Scanlins and the rest of the group, which he filled me in on later. The Scanlins had done as Russ advised and stayed to the woods. They hadn't come upon any others until they got to this area, when they ran into Mike Thomas, who was hunting for game to eat.

After the initial shock of finding each other, they shared their stories. Mike was a single guy, who worked nights. He had just gotten home when the grid went down. He told them he was with a group, but they didn't have much in the way of supplies. Sean relayed to Mike where they were trying to get to, the Callen farm, and suggested perhaps they work together to get there. Sean told him he couldn't say for certain that they would be able to stay, but the Callens had a large farm, and he felt there was room for more, if there weren't others already there. Mike asked about the rest of the group, and Sean said they could all travel together, since as a group they would be safer, and worry about the rest when they got there. Almost everyone in their group had handguns, rifles, and shotguns. This was Tennessee, after all. They did not have an abundance of ammo, though—maybe a thousand rounds total between all of them. Who needed to stockpile ammo? The sporting goods store was right down the road. Until SHTF—then, what you had was it.

Mike had told Sean that Ryan and Bill Lawton, the brothers, ran a landscaping service together. They had just pulled out with their truck and trailer when the pulse hit and stopped them dead in the road. Over the course of the day, they managed to push/pull the truck and trailer and get it back in their driveway, where it was still sitting. Pete and Sara Raines lived next door to Mike, and the Lawton brothers lived across the street. Lee Roush and his family lived next door to them. They hadn't been close friends before, but they were "talk across the fence" neighbors, and when everything went down, none of them had any long-term supplies. After the second day, they got together and checked empty houses on their street. There were quite a few. Unfortunately, it was a neighborhood full of young couples, who ate a lot of take out and microwavable food, and there wasn't a lot of that either. Being a prepper, I couldn't believe people lived with no more than a day or two of food in their house. If our house had been safe, or at least defendable, we could have easily lived a year or more off the food we had stored. But then I also thought: what would we have had if Russ hadn't made me see the light?

When Sean told Mike about the Callen farm, he took the Scanlin family back with him to their street. After a group meeting, they all decided they would try to get there together. They had literally just started out that morning, stopping where we found them to decide the best course of action and route to take. I'm a firm believer that everything happens for a reason. It was more than fate that they just happened to be there, with people we—well, Russ and Brian—knew, and pretty much heading the same way we were. Big question: how were we going to get eleven more people in our vehicles, which were already packed to the gills and then some? I knew we were going to take them with us—I just didn't know how we were going to do it.

I brought food and water down for the group. Russ had gone up to talk to Bob, to try to figure out how we could get them out to the Callen farm, or at least as far as our farm, and I went back up to join them.

Bob posed a question. "Are there any older vehicles in the area? Maybe we can find one, hot wire it, and they could use that. I mean, we might be able to take a couple more, if we dump a few things on the side of the road, and you might be able to take a couple in the bed of your truck, if they agree to hold a chicken pen. But there's no way we get them all in these two vehicles."

Russ thought for a second, then looked back down at the group. "They seem like good people. Lord knows there's going to be fewer and fewer of those around. The fact that they grouped up means they understand that they're stronger that way. I'd like to get them out to the Callen farm, or maybe even ours. We know we're going to need more people to secure it. Let's see if we can find another ride. In the meantime, let's back up and take the rigs down there. That way, we can all stay together, and these vehicles are not sitting up here for anybody to see."

They went to the trucks, backed up, and drove down the ramp. Everyone else walked down. Not knowing how long it would take to get to the farm, and how long we might be cooped up in the trucks, we took the opportunity to stretch our legs.

After they got the rigs down the ramp, Russ and Bob went to the guys in the group. "Do you guys know of any older cars or trucks, like ours, in the area? We want to take you with us, but we don't have room for this many people. If we could find an older truck or SUV, or even a station wagon, we could probably get everybody in, between the three."

The guys looked at each other, and Ryan and Bill seemed to think of something simultaneously. They both said at the same time, "Charlie!"

We all looked at them, not understanding. They grinned, and Bill filled us in. "Charlie Hotchkins lived on the other side of us. He was an old guy, and not very friendly. He was out west to see his kids and grandkids, though as crotchety as he was, I can't believe they wanted him to visit."

We all snickered, and he went on. "He has a, like, 1970 Ford LTD station wagon. The thing is a bus. It's covered up in his garage. Last time he cranked it, it ran like a champ. He did that at least once a month. Would that work?"

Russ smiled and nodded. "That would be perfect. Why didn't you guys think of that before?"

Bill had a sheepish look on his face. "I never thought about the older cars running. Everyone out by us had newer rides. I guess when I saw you guys in your trucks, something clicked in the back of my mind that the bus was out there and might run. We can walk back and get it—shouldn't take more than an hour."

Bob addressed Bill. "Do you know how to hot wire a car? I'm guessing you don't have a key for it."

Bill looked at Bob, then his brother, Ryan. "No, man, I got no idea how to do that. Do you guys know?"

Bob grinned at him. "Son, you might not have noticed, but we were kind of ready for something like this to happen. Hot wiring 101 was a required course for this event. I'm going to say we drop my trailer, grab some tools, and drive over. Sound good?"

They all agreed that was a great plan. Bob and Russ dropped Bob's trailer at the curb. Bob, Bill, Ryan, and Brian headed out to get the wagon. The rest of us stood, stretched, and got to know each other better. We already knew the Lawton brothers were landscapers. We learned Pete was a trucker, who had just gotten back the day before the pulse from a run, and wasn't due to head out again for two days. His wife, Sara, was a teacher, but Tony had been down with a cold, and she had called out that day to stay home and take care of him. Mike was a machinist, in a big factory in the city, and had literally just gotten home when the pulse hit. Lee was a carpenter, self-employed like Russ. His wife was an executive secretary and had been called in early for a board meeting for her boss. She would have been in the downtown area when the pulse hit, at least thirty miles away. In pumps and a business suit, I couldn't imagine she could have found a way to get home. Thirty miles might as well be three hundred without the right clothes and supplies, especially for a woman, alone, with no way to defend herself, in a lawless world. If she hadn't made it back by now, chances were slim to none she would. If she was still alive … I didn't want to think what her life might have become.

We finished lunch, and the kids were running around playing. Tony was thirteen, just a couple of years younger than our boys, so he chose to hang out with them over the younger kids. Aiden and Moira were already fast friends with Tara and Katlyn, so they had a game of tag going. We were watching them run around after each other when we heard a car, one we didn't recognize. Russ immediately grabbed his rifle and yelled for everyone to get to our truck and get down. The other men and our boys all pulled out handguns or rifles and ducked down beside the truck. Russ was watching down the street through the scope of his rifle. After a moment, in which I realized I was holding my breath, he stood up. He smiled back at us with a look of relief.

"It's okay. It's the wagon, and Bob is right behind them."

We all stood up, watching them come down the road. The wagon was not quiet, but it was not as loud as our trucks. It looked to be in pristine condition. Thank you, Charlie, wherever you are, for your contribution to the exodus effort. Ryan was driving, with a big grin on his face. He pulled up in front of Russ's truck.

"It's running, but there's not a lot of gas in it. Bob said you guys could help with that."

Russ nodded and went to the back of the trailer. He came back with two five-gallon gas cans. He handed them to Bill, who had gotten out and met him halfway. He went back to the wagon to fill it up. Bob parked behind the wagon and came over.

"Turns out, old Charlie had a key hanging inside the house. Yes, we broke in, but I figured it was better to have a key than to have to hot wire the thing every time to drive it."

We grinned at our goofy friend and waited for the Lawtons to get back over to us. Russ began to describe his plan.

"We can get maybe two more people in Bob's SUV, if we do some creative arranging, or just leave some stuff here. We can't put anyone else in our truck, unless they ride in the bed, and even then, they'll end up with a chicken or rabbit cage in their lap. I think you should be able to fit nine people in the wagon fine, as well as the few belongings you have with you. If we can do that, we can get back on the road and headed out to where we all seem to be going."

Mike and Bill offered to ride with Bob, and the rest of them worked out who was riding where in the wagon. It sounded like the kids were all going to be in the back, with the supplies they had been able to bring with them.

Russ continued. "I think we should put the wagon between the two rigs to convoy. The rigs are big and heavy and should provide protection for the lighter wagon, should someone try to get to it. So, if everyone is done with lunch and bathroom breaks, we should get this show on the road again. I really want to get to the farm today, well before dark, so we can get everything situated. We can check with Monroe, Janet's uncle, and see if he knows the Callens.

He's lived out there a long time, so if they are in the area, he'll know them. Then we can work out a plan to get you there, if you still want to go."

Sean looked confused. "Why wouldn't we still want to go, Russ?"

Russ smiled. "Well, our farm is pretty awesome, and we have room for more people, if any of you want to stay. We know we can't defend the whole place by ourselves and would have been out recruiting soon after we got there anyway. Also, you don't know if the Callens are at their place, not for sure. You don't know if something might have happened to their farm. You saw yourself how quickly a place can go up in flames and burn to the ground. I hope that hasn't happened, of course. I just want you to know you have options."

Sean nodded. "I see what you mean. Thank you for the offer, Russ. We'll definitely talk everything over when we get out there, and see what's what."

We loaded everyone up, making sure they were all situated in the wagon. Brian and Marietta got to be pretty cozy in the SUV, but it didn't look like they minded. With everyone ready, we headed up the ramp to get back on the highway. The next hour or so should see us getting to the farm, barring any problems. I hoped and prayed there wouldn't be any.

# Chapter 20

We got about five miles down the road before we saw anybody. Honestly, I was surprised when we did. There were a lot less cars on the road, especially heading south, away from town. But there they were—four guys, with an old pickup with a camper on it, parked sideways across the road, up against an old van, in a vain attempt to block the southbound lanes of the highway. I say vain attempt, because you could easily take the shoulder on the right and pass their "roadblock." I looked at Russ, who looked at me, and we both kind of smirked at the set up. To their credit, they were lined up in front of the vehicles with what appeared to be 12-gauge shotguns at the ready. They could have been a force, but we had them outnumbered, shooter-wise, by about three to one. Russ pulled up to a stop, about a hundred feet from them. He pulled out the radio and hailed Bob.

"Are you seeing this?"

Bob came back quickly. "Yeah, buddy. We can take them, pretty easy, but I don't want to take the chance of anyone getting caught by a stray shot, not on our side anyway. What do you want to do?"

Russ replied, "I want us to get out of our vehicles slowly, with whatever weapon is closest, in a show of force. Don't point anything at them, but make sure they see it. Keep the kids in the cars, ours included. We'll have Ben and Rusty hold up a long gun, to show them that everyone is armed. Can you let the others know?"

We didn't have a radio for the wagon, so we would have to go over and let them know what was happening and what the plan was. Bob said he'd take care of it right away. We got out of our truck, with our handguns out, but pointed down. Bob got out of his and went over to the wagon. I stayed by the door of the truck; Russ moved out to the front of it, but stopped there. Kind of marking his territory, without going to the trouble to pee on the tires.

The guys from the roadblock moved forward, covering about a third of the distance between us. They were dirty, with what looked to be chewing tobacco spittle stains on their clothes. I couldn't see them fully well, but they seemed to be lacking in the teeth area. Their spokesperson kept coming, slowly walking toward us.

"Where y'all headed?" He finished his statement by spitting a stream of tobacco juice to the pavement. Classy.

Russ affected the same Southern drawl. "Oh, 'bout ten, twenty miles down the road. Got some kin down that way, hopin' they can put us up."

The spokesman continued. "What y'all got in them thar trailers?"

Russ waved them off. "Aw, nuthin' but clothes and beds and stuff. Our kin won't have anythin' like that for us."

"Mind if we take a look? We're tryin' to keep this area safe from dangerous folks, and we want to make sure y'all ain't dangerous."

Russ raised his pistol and pointed it at the guy. He cleaned up his accent quick. "As a matter of fact, I do mind. What we have is none of your business. Now, move those vehicles out of the road, so we can be on our way, or we'll move them ourselves."

The guy stopped in his tracks. His buddies raised their shotguns and pointed them at Russ. At the same time, Bob, Brian, and the rest of the guys stepped out and up beside us with handguns, rifles, and shotguns pointed their way. The men down the road looked at our guys, did the math, and lowered their weapons. The spokesman lowered his as well, but was still trying to keep the upper hand.

"Well, we got to charge you a toll to use this road. What ya gonna pay with?"

Russ smiled at him. "Has something changed in the past couple of weeks? This road is not a toll road. Even if it were, the toll would not be collected by the likes of you. Now, back off, move those vehicles, and leave us to go on our way—before one, or all of you, gets hurt."

The speaker looked confused, like he wasn't exactly sure what to do next. Were we the first people to challenge them? Sad. He tried to continue down the path he had started.

"Now, look here. Ever-body pays the toll. Whatever ya got that's worth somethin' will do. Food, guns, ammo, women …"

At the last comment, Janet and I both raised our sidearms and leveled them at his head. I took the lead.

"Are you trying to tell me you have been traded women for passage on this road?"

I almost screamed it at him, so no doubt his cohorts heard it as well. I pulled the hammer back on my pistol. He held up his hands.

"No! No! No one has traded any women to pass through here. We just want to make sure ever-body knows all the options they have. No offense, ma'am."

As he tried hard to cover his tracks, I kept my pistol pointed at his head. "Offense taken. You will get nothing from us! Now back the fuck off!" Oh, I used the F-bomb. Yep, I was pissed.

I started toward him, with my gun pointed at his head. Russ intercepted me. "Easy, babe. I've got this."

Probably a good thing, because I wanted nothing more than to shoot Tobacco Spitter in the face at that moment. Russ placed his hand over the top of my pistol and gently pushed it down toward the ground. I let him. I released the hammer back to the at rest position, but kept it pointed in the shit heel's general direction.

Russ stepped forward, with his own pistol pointed down but toward the guy. "Look, I don't know why you haven't figured it out yet, but we are not giving you anything. Now, I'm going to tell you one more time to get those vehicles out of the road, or else."

Dumbass decided to get lippy. "Or else what? Ya gonna just shoot us, right here, on the road, out in the open?"

Russ brought his pistol up and pointed it at the redneck's head. "That's exactly what we're going to do. So, you need to ask yourself—is this really worth dying for? I have no qualms about leaving your rotting corpse right here in the middle of the road and driving over it. What'll it be?"

I guess the idiot finally figured out we were serious, because he held both hands up and started backing toward his buddies. "Uh, sure, no problem, we'll get the road opened up right real quick for ya. Sorry for any inconvenience we might have caused."

He kept walking backward, keeping us in his line of sight, until he got to the blockade. He said something we couldn't hear to the other men, and two of them jumped in and started the vehicles up, then backed them off the center of the road.

Russ spoke to us over his shoulder. "Anne, you drive our truck through. I'll walk beside on the driver's side, and we'll have Mike man the other side. Pete can drive the wagon, and we'll have Bill and Ryan walk beside that. Janet will drive their SUV, with Bob and Brian walking that one. I want eyes on these assholes at all times, as each vehicle gets through, and for at least a hundred yards past them, before we load up again. I'll stop when we are all through and I think we're far enough to be clear."

We all headed for our appointed places and got the cars going. I had the lead and drove slowly toward the now cleared section of road. As we passed, the men were giving us dirty looks—one flipped me off. Really, dude? We have armed men everywhere and you want to cop an attitude? I just shook my head, flipped him off in response, and laughed.

We got past them, and once Janet got their rig through, the dirt bags closed up their "roadblock" again. Bob had walked the length of his rig, so that he was behind it when Janet finally cleared the cars. He walked backward, keeping them in his sight the whole time. The spokesman looked like he was going to follow us, but Bob brought his shotgun up and pointed it at him.

"Stop right there, fella. You've managed to live through this so far, don't screw up now. We'll be on our way now, unless you want to get stupid here at the end." The idiot stopped, started to raise his shotgun, but by then Brian and the Lawton brothers were back there with Bob. He pointed his gun back to the ground. Good boy.

Russ had seen the interaction from the right side, and he motioned me to keep going. We ended up a good quarter of a mile from them before we stopped—way out of shotgun range. By then, all the guys walking were grouped up behind Bob's trailer, still keeping an eye on the rednecks, who looked to still be eyeballing us but seemed to be losing interest.

Russ met up with the guys after we stopped. He looked at Bob. "We good? Do we need to go back and get any points across?"

Bob shook his head. "Nah, I think they got the message. Let's get to the farm. We are literally like ten minutes away!"

He was bouncing around like a pinball, and the guys all laughed at his actions.

"Okay, buddy, let's get to the farm." Russ turned and headed back to our rig.

We were almost there. I was excited too—we all were. We just had to get about two more miles down the highway, then another five across to the farm. I could almost taste Millie's biscuits and gravy already.

# Chapter 21

We didn't run into any trouble on the rest of the trip down the highway. There were a few abandoned cars, but none that stopped us from getting through. Once we got off the highway onto the road that would take us out to the farm, things changed. This was a two-lane road, and not very wide. Not a half-mile down it there was a big dually pickup sitting in our lane, and it had hit a mid-sized SUV in the other lane. Great. Now what? There wasn't room to go around on either side. Russ pulled up to a stop, and the rest of our caravan did the same. We got out to inspect the scene. Mike, the trucker, walked up to the pickup and looked in.

"Well, the good news is the keys are still here."

Rusty looked at his dad, clearly confused. "Why is that good news, Dad? It won't run, right? If it did, whoever owns it wouldn't have left it, would they?"

Russ nodded. "That's right, son, but even though it won't run, the key engages or disengages the mechanical aspects of the transmission. So even though we can't start it, we can put it in neutral, so we can push it out of the way."

Mike had opened the door and climbed in to do just that. He turned to us and motioned us over. Looking into the SUV, we could see that there was blood on the seat.

"You might want to keep the kids back," Mike said. "I'm not sure what happened, but it looks like they might have been close to passing each other when this went down, and the SUV swerved a bit into this truck."

As well as the blood, the windshield was smashed. Looked like someone had hit it with their head. There was not a body though, so apparently they had been able to walk out of there. Head wounds bleed profusely, and because of that, a lot of the time they look worse than they really are.

With no signs of a body, Russ and I went around to the driver's side. No keys in this one. You bust your head on the windshield and think to take your keys when you leave? Russ stood back up and looked over at everyone else.

"Well, the bad news is, this one does not have keys. It's going to be a bitch to move, and we're going to have to move it first. Good thing we have all these folks with us."

Mike was still looking the situation over. "Russ, your truck is a hoss. If you drop your trailer, I'm betting you can push that SUV out of the way, with our help, even if it is in gear. What do you think?"

Russ looked at the vehicles, then his truck. "Well, there's a reason I put that push bar on the front. Let's give it a try."

Russ went back to the trailer hitch and dropped the trailer. He pulled up to the front corner of the SUV and rolled up until the truck was against it. He put it in park, got out, and went around to look and see what was needed to get it moved. The rest of the guys were standing by, awaiting instructions.

"I think if I push slow but firm and you guys find a spot somewhere along the sides you can grab and help, this might work. Let's see what happens. Everybody be careful though—we can't afford for anyone to get run over, or cut, or anything like that."

All the men lined up on both sides of the SUV as Russ got back in his truck. He started it up, put it in gear, and gave it some gas. The engine revved, and at first we didn't think it was going to work, but the SUV slowly started moving. It was still putting a strain on our truck, but we had to do it. There was only one road to the farm, and this was it.

The guys pushed on the sides until Russ had gotten the front free from the dually, then some of them moved to the hood and pushed from there. It was much better leverage, and the SUV picked up a bit of speed—well, a few more inches per minute anyway. After about ten minutes, the SUV was off the side of the road in the ditch. Sorry, missing SUV owner, but not running in the ditch off the road is no worse than not running in the middle of the road, for you anyway. Since Russ was already unhooked from the trailer, they used our truck to push the dually off the road as well. Much faster and easier when you could take it out of gear and actually steer it. That one went in the ditch on the other side of the road.

Russ took the opportunity to run down the road and around the corner, to see if there were any other obstacles ahead. He was back in just a couple of minutes.

"Looks like we've got a clear shot for at least the next mile. A couple of cars, but they are off to the side, so we can shoot down the middle of the road. Let's get going."

****

We got the trailer hooked back up and headed out. I wondered what had happened to the people in those vehicles. They both had local tags, so hopefully they hadn't been too far from home and had been able to get back. Back to what, though? Had they planned for something like this? Did they have supplies? Two weeks ago I would have seen a scene like this and just wondered if they had survived the crash, especially the SUV driver. Now, the crash was almost an afterthought. Strange, how your perspective changes to match the reality of your world.

We went two more miles before the road was blocked again, but this time it was just a small car that seemed to have died and drifted to the middle of the road. Russ stopped and got out to have a look.

He no sooner got to the car than a man and woman popped up from the other side, both with guns. The man had what looked like a .357 revolver, and the woman was sporting a shotgun. They pointed the guns at Russ, who stopped in his tracks. I stifled a scream. He closed his eyes and tipped his head down, while raising his hands in the air. I knew what he was thinking: *Dumb move, Russ. You know better. You should have looked around before you got out.* We were so close to the farm, less than two miles, so I could understand the excitement and the rush to get there making him less cautious.

The man spoke first. "We'll be taking that rig you got there, mister. Have your family get out real slow and step away. No reason for anyone to die here, over a truck and trailer. We don't want to hurt anyone; we just need whatever you got in there."

Russ looked at the man. "Buddy, I could be hauling trash in that trailer for all you know. How do you know you 'need' it? Besides that, has it completely escaped your notice that there are two more vehicles behind mine, all full of people with guns pointed at you both as we speak? Did you have a plan for dealing with all of us, or did you think you could just pick us off one by one and not get yourselves killed? Because you should know, everyone you see holding a gun can shoot, and can shoot well. You start shooting, you will die. Is that what you want?"

As Russ was delivering this speech, all the guys from the wagon and Bob's SUV stepped out with handguns, shotguns, and rifles, all pointed at the couple. I had already gotten out with my pistol aimed at the missus. Either they just weren't paying attention to what was behind us—maybe they didn't expect to see that many vehicles that still ran together—or they were so desperate they didn't care.

Just when I thought Russ was going to talk them down, the man fired a shot from his revolver. It was pointed in Russ's direction, but downward, so the bullet went to Russ's right side and hit the road. It didn't matter though. Once he fired, the rest of us opened up. They were down in a matter of seconds. It was a complete reflex. They had guns pointed at my husband, at me, at my son, and I did not hesitate for a second once I heard the shot. Neither did Bob, or most of the guys. We didn't know if he'd fired intentionally, or by accident, and we did not have the luxury of time to find out. Like I said, it didn't matter.

Russ held up his hand and yelled, "Cease fire! They're down!"

He walked over, pistol drawn, and moved to the other side of the now bullet-riddled car. The man and woman were lying on the ground in a large pool of their combined blood. Russ closed his eyes, placed his head in his hands, and stood like that for a minute.

I didn't know what to do. Should I go to him, console him? It wasn't his fault—he was trying to keep anything like this from happening. The man probably shot by accident, which was why we were all ingrained to keep our finger off the trigger until we were ready to actually shoot. There was no way to know what his intentions had been. Taking the time to try to talk after a shot was fired is a good way to get dead. I had tears running down my cheeks. We had killed two people. Two desperate, dumb people, but two people nonetheless. Did they have kids they had left hidden somewhere, who were now orphans? Lord, I hoped not. As I was debating with myself whether to go to Russ or wait for him to come back, Mike walked over to him. Strange, since he was so new to our group. He laid a hand on Russ's shoulder and spoke softly to him, though I was close enough to hear what he said.

"When I was in Iraq, one of the first skirmishes I was involved in was a woman and a child, set up on the side of the road with what appeared to be a disabled car. We stopped to help, and as soon as we opened the doors to the hummer to check on them, they blew up themselves, the car, and two of our team. I knew they had brought it on themselves, and I knew they had tried to kill us, but it didn't stop me from having nightmares about it for months after. It was the first time I saw a dead body, and I don't think you ever forget that. You did nothing wrong. We did nothing wrong. They did this. I know you're feeling a little bit of everything right now, but we really need to get going, in case they were with anyone else and someone heard our gunshots. We don't need to even take time to bury them. We need to move them and the car off the road and get out of here. I can deal with the bodies, if you want me to."

Russ didn't say anything, but nodded in agreement. Mike proceeded to drag the man's body to the side of the road. We were all in shock over what had happened, and seeing Mike dragging the bodies of people who had been speaking to us just minutes before was a very surreal moment for me. He dragged the woman next and placed her beside the man.

"Do we have a tarp, or a sheet to spare? Something we can at least cover the bodies with?"

Mike's question was directed at the group, but I took the lead. "Let me get a sheet from our gear."

I went back to our trailer and grabbed the first sheet I found. In TEOTWAWKI, who cares if the sheets match?

I handed the sheet to Mike, and in the process couldn't help but see the bodies. I don't know what I expected to feel, but I instantly teared up again. So stupid. If you had just kept your finger off the trigger, this wouldn't have happened. Why didn't you try asking for help, before resorting to this behavior? Is this the world now? Nobody even tries to work things out? Or had the world gotten to this point in just a week, while we were still at home planning our exodus? Why did man always go to taking from others by force, before they even tried to make it on their own? Or had they tried and not been able to live? Not everyone knew how to hunt and clean game if they did happen to get something. Most people had no idea how many edible plants grow wild. Honestly, until a few years ago, neither did I. Even then, I was reliant on books to refer to so I would know what we could safely forage if needed. Things that our ancestors knew from experience we had lost because we didn't need to know it anymore. Look at us now.

Mike covered the bodies, and the guys got together and pushed the car out of the way. Mike went to Russ. "Are you okay to drive?"

Russ gave him a small smile. "We are spitting distance from the farm. Yes, I can make it."

He headed back toward our truck and motioned to the group. "Load up, gang. We are almost there. Let's go see the farm."

# Chapter 22

Russ was quiet as he drove. I knew him well enough to know he felt terrible, and probably partially responsible for those people being dead. I had to say something.

"Baby, what happened was not your fault. You were trying to talk them down. He obviously fired inadvertently—I mean, no warning, no escalation of the situation—it had to be an accident. It is not your fault he had his finger on the trigger. It is not your fault he fired. It is not your fault the rest of us fired back. You could not have prevented this. Stop beating yourself up over it. Please."

Russ looked at me, eyes full of pain. "I know. Every word you just said is true. I know it's not my fault. I know you all reacted as you should have. It still doesn't ease the pain in my heart. I knew we would probably have to take lives at some point during this new reality. I just wasn't mentally ready for it yet. It hasn't even been two weeks. I can't believe society has stooped so low so fast. It's worse than any scenario I had thought of or planned for. I'm afraid we are going to be in for a lot more of this kind of thing at the farm. We have to get there, get settled in, and get busy on security and reinforcements. The bad is coming, fast."

I nodded my head in sad agreement. I wasn't ready for it to be this ugly yet either. All we could do was hope that the farm was far enough away from civilization that we could stave off the ugly for a little while.

Russ took the next left, which was more of a cow path than a road, and headed into what looked like the woods. There was nothing but trees for as far as the eye could see. We rounded the corner, and Russ let a smile creep onto his face.

"We're here."

From the road, if you didn't know it was there, you would never see the entrance to the place. It was completely camouflaged with trees and brush that were actually attached to the gate. The trees were artificial, but they were very high quality, and you had to get up next to them and actually touch the leaves to find that out. Russ, Bob, and Monroe had spent hours working on it and checking it from every angle on the road to make sure no one could tell it was actually a gate. It was heavy, and the guys had offered to try to lighten the load for him, but Monroe had waved them off.

"We don't leave here but about once a month to go to town, and even then we don't really have to; we just do it to keep adding to the supplies while we can. I can handle it for no more than that."

It looked just like it had when we had been there a few weeks ago, which was a good sign. If someone had found the place, chances are they wouldn't have taken the time to reset the gate if they had busted it in, which they would have had to do—as I said, it's heavy—and the same camouflage lined either side of it for a quarter of a mile. This was the front edge of the property. The rest was extra-high barbed-wire fenced, but even that was set back into the trees a good hundred feet, and Mother Nature was allowed to grow whatever her heart desired between the fence and the edge of the property. You couldn't see the fence from outside the property, and the tree line was so thick there was nothing that would let an outsider know there was any reason to go deeper in.

Russ pulled up about a hundred feet from it and stopped. The rest of the convoy pulled in behind us. He got out, looking all around for anyone who might be watching. He pulled out his binoculars and checked in all directions. Bob had a set and was looking as well. I looked back at the group; Mike had a set out, doing the same. We were going to have to figure out how to keep him. Former military, whether a prepper or not, he was adapting quickly to this new world. He had experience and skills we could use immediately, and apparently some valuable supplies. We would need more like him to defend the farm. I made a mental note to bring that up with Russ at the first opportunity.

Russ signaled that it was clear, and everyone exited the vehicles and headed our way. Russ addressed the group.

"We're here, gang. We just need to signal Monroe that it's us, so he doesn't shoot us, then it's about a half-mile in to the homestead. As I said before, you are more than welcome to stay with us for the duration, but I hope you will at least stay a night or two, so you can get some decent rest and solid food, and get a plan in place. We knew all along we were never going to defend this place with just the eight of us, and we have plenty of room to create more shelters. Knowing Monroe, he probably has the supplies to build a bunch of tiny houses."

Bob spoke up. "He does. I've seen it. The man collects everything and throws nothing out. I swear, he has pieces of Noah's Ark stashed somewhere."

We all laughed until Russ went on. "So, there's your validation. What I'm trying to say is you are welcome to stay, for as long as you like. If you decide to leave"—he was looking at the Scanlins—"we'll do whatever we can to help you on your way. No one has to make any decisions right away. Let's get up to the house and check on Monroe and Millie, and get this next chapter started."

Janet and I looked at each other and grinned. We were so excited to see them again. Honestly, they were the grandparents none of us had anymore. Russ and Bob went to the fence. Bob had a black case in his hand; he opened it and pulled out a flare gun. This was our signal to Monroe that it was us. Not many people carry flare guns with them, so we were pretty sure this method would be safe enough. However, there was more to the signal code. Monroe had to reply back, using a mirror to signal Morse code. He sent, "Password." Russ signaled back, "Molon labe." Monroe then fired his own signal flare. We were clear to enter. Overkill? Maybe, but it was the best we civilians could come up with when we were deciding what to do if SHTF.

Bob unlocked the padlock on the gate, and Russ and the rest of the guys helped him open it up. We drove the vehicles through quickly, then the guys all jumped back out, ran to the gate, and closed and locked it back up. Once we were sure it was secured again, we headed in to the farmhouse. What a welcome sight Millie and Monroe were, standing on the porch, fit as could be at their age! All the dogs were with them, paying attention, but they recognized our vehicles, so they were calm. I was so excited to see them I was jumping in the seat.

Russ looked at me and grinned an evil grin. "Should I slow down, take my time getting up there?"

I punched him in the arm. "No! Hurry up!"

He laughed out loud—thank goodness, he was coming back to his old self—and headed toward the front stoop. He stopped just before it, and I was out before he even got the truck in park. I ran up to them and threw my arms around both of them at the same time.

"You're here! You're safe! We were so worried about you!"

They both hugged me back, and then I stepped out of the way for the rest of the family to greet them. I had tears running down my face. What was that about? Joy? Relief? Probably both, and a lot more. It took us about five minutes to get through the families hugging each other and the dogs getting their petting as well, then

Monroe stepped out and looked at the rest of the group standing in the yard, looking a bit awkward.

"Been collecting, I see," he said to Russ.

Russ nodded. "Yes, and I think we have done well so far."

Millie stepped around the men and walked to the group. "Welcome to our home, all of you. Please make yourselves at home, wherever you can find a spot. We'll figure out the sleeping arrangements later, but for now, let's get some food in you."

Gotta love a gracious Southern woman. The rest of the group started walking toward the house, shaking hands with them both, then spreading out in the yard and on the porch, just enjoying a "home" again. The dogs went around to each person, sniffing to get to know their scents. Since they had all come in with us, they were accepted as new members of the pack. Rusty and Ben kept their eyes on them, to make sure the smaller kids weren't scared.

Moira came up to me and asked if the bathroom worked. I bent down to her level and smiled. "It does, but we have to help it flush. Come on, I'll show you where it is and how it works."

The great thing about a septic tank—it isn't dependent on technology. It just needs water to wash it down.

Russ looked at me as I was walking by. "Is there anything dire we need to get unloaded?"

"The only things we need to get out are the animals. We should be able to add them to the pens here, but I'd set them inside the enclosures, in their cages, for now, just to see how everyone gets along. With all of ours being female, there shouldn't be any testosterone flaring up, but sometimes estrogen can be just as bad. Not that you'd know anything about that, huh, baby?" I smiled sweetly at him.

He shook his head. "Uh uh—no way I'm stepping into that one. Rusty! Ben! Come help me with these critters!"

Ryan and Bill jumped up. "What do you need, Russ? We can help. We need to start earning our keep around here." Ryan was talking, but Bill was nodding his head while his brother spoke.

Russ looked at them. "There will be plenty of time, and plenty to do, for everyone around here to earn their keep very soon, but if you want, grab a cage out of my truck."

Mike walked up without saying a word and grabbed one as well. Yeah, I really, really liked him.

When Moira and I came back down, I sent her out to play with the dogs and the other kids, and I went to the kitchen to help with the food. I found Janet, Marietta, Kate, and Sara in there as well. Good thing it was a big country kitchen. Kate and Sara seemed to be working on plates, utensils, and glasses, while Janet and Millie were warming up leftovers. There was a ton of food, already cooked. I was shocked.

"Millie, why did you have all this food cooked already? You couldn't have known we'd be here today, and certainly not with all these people. There's enough food to feed everybody and still have leftovers."

Millie looked at me and smiled. "I'm not sure, Anne. I woke up this morning, and I told Monroe: 'We're going to have company today. A lot of company. We need to get some food cooked.' So, I started cooking. All we have to do now is heat it up. Something or someone was telling me y'all were coming today. I've got a feeling I know who." Millie looked completely peaceful, not a worry in the world, and she turned back to the stove.

"Okay, then what can I do?"

She said over her shoulder, "Get those men and kids to wash up out at the pump house. I left soap and towels out there this morning." Psychic Millie was scary, but efficient.

I walked out the front door. There were people everywhere. Kids running and playing with the dogs; men watching the chickens interact through the cages; more men checking the place out; and Russ, Bob, Brian, and Monroe off by themselves. That couldn't be good. I hollered to the group in general.

"Hey, everybody! Millie has an awesome dinner waiting for us. Y'all go over to the pump house and get washed up. Rusty and Ben can show you where it is."

Russ and company started my way. I met them in the yard. "What's up? What were you guys talking about?"

Russ looked at me grimly. "We'll talk at dinner. Let's put the kids in the screen porch, so the adults can talk."

So, I was right. Not good.

****

Monroe took the lead at dinner. "The first thing I did once we figured out the power was out was check my old truck and tractor. They both still ran. I took the truck into town and found out real quick there wasn't much else running. I got some looks from some folks at the general store when I went to buy up the flour, sugar, salt, and a few other things I could with the cash I had. I saw a couple of punks eyeballing my truck, so I headed back here. Problem was, those punks know us, though I don't think they know where we live. They haven't shown up yet, but I expect they will at some point. Good thing is it's a good ten miles to town. I imagine they'll get here sooner or later. I doubt they'll be alone."

Russ spoke up. "We're going to need to start security watches immediately. Yes, it's been over a week since Monroe was in town, but there is no doubt we will be discovered here by someone. Right now, we have enough bodies that we can do two-hour shifts, two per shift, and still have people left over. I think that will work for now. We just want to make sure someone is awake at all times, to give us a heads up if they see or hear anything. We can work up a schedule of all who would like to volunteer for a shift."

Russ paused as every person at the table raised a hand, including the women. He nodded and smiled. "I had a feeling about this group. Thank you all."

Rusty came running in from the screen porch. "Dad! I heard something! I think it was a four-wheeler, out in the area of the road!"

Everyone jumped up, grabbed the closest weapon, and rushed out the front door. We stopped and listened. Yes, it was definitely a four-wheeler, out on the road.

Russ looked at Monroe. "Have you heard any vehicles out here since everything went down?"

Monroe shook his head. "Only ours. Makes sense a four-wheeler would run—more like a motorcycle, probably manual start."

We stood still, listening to the motor fade away. We breathed a collective sigh of relief, but Russ had a serious look on his face.

"That settles it. We start security watches tonight. Also, keep lanterns and candle flames low, and no more daytime fires. Everybody who is not on watch tonight, get a good night's sleep, because first thing in the morning, we unpack everything we brought, get settled, and get busy. We need to work on shelter for the new folks and figure out how to get Sean and Kate to their friends' house, if they still want to go."

Sean looked at Kate, then at Russ. "I think we should stay here for now, if that's okay. I don't want to take my family right back out on the road. They need some rest and a safe place to sleep, at least for a few days. If that's okay with everyone."

Russ nodded. "More than okay. I'm glad you decided to stay, at least for a while. Let's get inside, gang. We need to get ready for the tomorrows that are coming, and the bad people that are bringing them.

The story continues in *When the Peace is Gone*

# Acknowledgments

Thank you to all of you who have purchased my first novel. I hope you enjoyed it and I hope you will want to read the rest of their story.

I never thought about writing a novel. Well, okay, I thought about it, but I didn't know what I would write about. What did I have to offer the world that people would want to read? When I got the idea for *When the Power is Gone*, it was like someone had flipped a switch in me. I started writing and after about six chapters I had my husband take a look. His excitement at wanting to know the rest of the story spurred me on. The finished product is something I'm proud of.

So, I'll start off by thanking my husband, Jim, for his unwavering support of me in this endeavor. He built my website, and keeps it updated with new reviews and content. He was my first proofreader. He pushed me to stay with it, and finish it. He gave me the time I needed to work on it, even if it changed plans we had made for something else. He has shared every joy with me as we have watched the ratings rise on the initial version. He is my best friend and the inspiration behind this book. Thank you, baby.

I would also like to thank my aunt, Carol. Her help with reading my work-in-progress and information on writing methods made me totally revamp the first version. Thank you, sweet aunt.

Thank you to all of my friends who were some of the first to read it (and they paid for it, I did not give it to them for free), who sent me messages about how much they loved the book and couldn't wait for the next installment. Kim, Jeana, Christy—thank you for the encouragement.

I want to thank all the other authors in this genre. This is a field that is pretty much male dominated, as far as the writers go. I've read dozens of books they've written and they go into great detail about weapons, logistics, and machismo. I got the idea to write this book because of that. I wanted to try to write one from a woman's perspective; one more like myself, who found her world completely changed in a matter of seconds, and how she could and would adapt to it. I think I accomplished that.

Lastly, I want to thank the Lord for the gift he gave me of wit, words, and a desire to do something I'd never done before. I placed my life in His hands and all I have is because of Him. Thank you, Lord, for the many blessings you bestow upon me every day.

Find us on the web!

The website is always updating, so keep coming back for more info.
Want to stay up to date on all our latest news? Join our mailing list!

www.paglaspy.com

Facebook: facebook.com/paglaspy

Twitter: @paglaspy

Goodreads: P.A. Glaspy

Made in the USA
Coppell, TX
21 September 2020